Meliu
Sundering the Gods:
Book 1.5

by

L. James Rice

Meliu is a work of fiction. Names, characters, places, and incidents are the product of the author's imagination or are used fictitiously. Any resemblance to actual events, locales, or persons, living, dead, undead, possessed, or anywhere in between is purely coincidental.

Cover design by Damonza.com
Cartography by Jenna Jing Rice

ISBN: 978-1-7324083-9-5 Paperback
ISBN: 978-1-7324083-3-3 Ebook
ISBN: 978-1-7324083-4-0 Hardback

Join the Sundering the Gods newsletter list for updates,
promotions, and exclusive short works at:
sunderingthegods.com

Dedicated to my lovely wife and two beautiful daughters;
may their inspiration live forever.

TERRITORY OF THE CLAN CHOERKIN

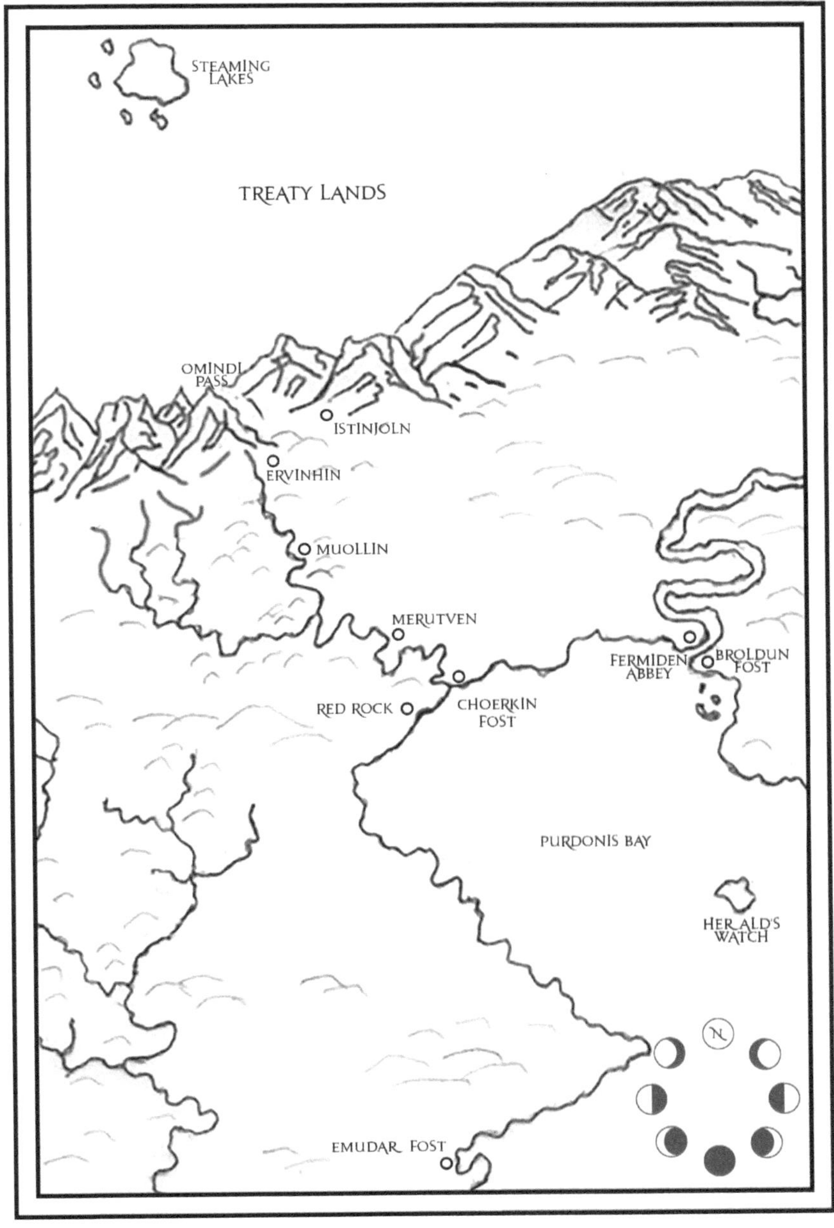

THE SUNDERING THE GODS SAGA

EVE OF SNOWS
MELIU
TRAIL OF PYRES
SOLINEUS
CITY OF WHISPERS

Join the Sundering the Gods Newsletter At:

www.LJamesrice.com

Signed Editions Available at
L. James Rice's Facebook page, or email:
LJRice@SunderingTheGods.com

If you enjoy Meliu, please consider leaving a review at your favorite online retailer.

FOREWARD

The Evolution of Meliu

Meliu started Eve of Snows as a minor character, her destiny to retrieve a book and return it to Istinjoln, never to be seen again. Heck, we weren't even supposed to meet her in Chapter One! But as the book came together, Meliu kept inserting herself into the future of the story. She's kind of pushy that way. With her growing importance, I decided to bump the girl Tokodin originally gambled with in order to replace her with Meliu, so we'd meet this beautiful priestess right up front.

About the same time as this change was made, an epiphany struck: She would be a major player in book two, a Point of View character. This felt a little odd, since she disappears in Chapter 25/26 and we have no idea how she reaches Book Two, Trail of Pyres, when it starts.

No big deal, right? Just plug in a bunch of exposition and be on your way. That's how it started, and it probably would've worked, but the deeper I got into Trail, the more fleshing out her journey made sense. And the more cool tidbits I could bring out.

Another big factor in writing 1.5 is that Meliu takes off like a shot in Trail of Pyres, at least in respect to her character arc. Yes, we met

Meliu in Eve of Snows, but we weren't in her head, and didn't really get to know her. Therefore, it made sense to give the reader a chance to get to know her like I do, before she begins her transformation, and to do that without slowing down Trail of Pyres' story.

So, prepare to travel back in time, so we may again move forward. I hope you enjoy getting to know Meliu as much as I have.

One

A Scar Lost

Talons plunge, unfurled wings, storm clouds blow,
slow, the flow, the fall of the reign amidst the rain,
strike the eye and emblazon the beak,
death first takes the timid and weak.
Feed and fed, the eagle leaves you dead,
be thankful to never know the vulture's breath.

—*Tomes of the Touched*

Seven Days to the Eve of Snows

Meliu handed the Codex of Sol to Woxlin with profound pride and loss. For days she'd dreamed of a glance into the relic's pages, but its lock confounded her. She'd learned from her mother how to slip past a lock on the Raging Dragon's liquor stores at an inappropriate age, only months before being shipped to Istinjoln on her fifth birthday. Locks abounded in Istinjoln, guarding famous brew or forbidden libraries, but not one she dared defied her.

The tiny tumblers on an invaluable manuscript thwarted her efforts.

And now it sat in a high priest's hands, his knuckles whitening with an iron grip. She smiled at his crooked teeth set in a crooked grin, unable to look him in the eye. A priest with their face buried in a bowed cowl stood to his side holding a lantern, and Woxlin held out the tome for this other to take, and whispered: "For Lord Priest Ulrikt, immediately."

The other nodded. A feminine hand with fingers long enough to grasp the thick tome with confidence snatched its bindings and shoved it beneath the folds of her robes. This priestess disappeared with long strides as Woxlin held Meliu's cheeks with both hands and kissed her forehead, his lips forming into a smirk after. "Get yourself to the healers, my girl."

Meliu trotted after the other priestess without so much as a glance back at the Choerkin and Wardens, catching a door to a small outbuilding before it closed. But the room was already empty. She glanced into the hollow shadows and set her gaze on the trapdoor in the floor. "What in the hells?" The priestess must've passed straight through the next door and closed it behind her, or she was shittin' quick. And in a hurry. *If she knows what she carries, I don't blame her.*

She tugged the rope on the trapdoor and eased down the ladder, nodding to a young monk's bow before realizing she didn't know where she was going. The Hall of Erginle, where healers practiced their arts during the day, would be empty after sundown. Any young priest dedicated to Life might improve the mending of her scalp, but with Little Sister's herbs and her own half-baked healing already having built layers of scars, she needed experienced prayer.

Meliu'd always been pretty, beautiful some said. The notion of folks looking at her ugly scar didn't wrench her gut, or so she tried to convince herself, it was the pity she expected to see in their eyes for what she'd lost.

She recalled her bloody-fisted pa standing above a man groggy on his hands and knees, streams of blood from his nose and mouth: "If you pity a man ya'd might as well be pissin' on 'im." Trime kicked the beleaguered man in the face and drug him out of the inn to lie in the dirt street where local miners laughed and urinated on the poor bastard. Insulting Trime's cooking was one thing, if done with a smile, but taking pity on all the miners who had to eat his cooking wasn't a trifle her pa took as a joke.

Meliu didn't have a lot of memories of her father before she moved to Istinjoln, but every one left their mark on her attitude, good or bad.

She huffed as she tromped down the hall. Pity was only good when it was a tool, and even then hard to stomach. She fought angry tears by the time she reached the Hall of Erginle and screamed when the lanterns hanging from the walls revealed no one. The echoes of her voice faded, and she wandered crest-fallen to the Goddess' shrine, staring at the stone beneath her feet. Her eyes rose to gaze upon the Tree of Life, the constellation of Erginle, here depicted by polished oak inlaid into the granite wall and set with twenty round diamonds, all bigger than her eyes.

"You've done well, my child."

The voice came from behind and she recognized the tones. She didn't turn to face her Lord Priest, she knelt, eyes pinned on the highest diamond in the tree. "Have I? I wonder."

Ulrikt strode in front of her and turned so she stared into his eyes. Soft blue, caring, but without pity. "A frightful wound." His fingers brushed the bulge of her scar.

"There're Shadows at the Shrine." But he knew already; she felt foolish.

He leaned like a tree in a strong breeze, his palm covering the side of her head. "We shan't worry about Shadows this evening, shall we, my girl?" He smiled, and tingles wove into the scars hugging her skull, wiggling through the muscles of her face so close to her nose she fought the urge to sneeze. "We will contain the Shadows as before, destroy them if need be."

If need be? You shittin' me? "As you say, my Lord Priest."

"You have questions. I understand. But you must trust in me, and trust in Sol, and in his Codex."

Heat flared through every creeping tingle in her head, but she forced herself calm until the threat of a pain that never quite came faded. He stood straight, a cocksure grin on his face. As the beat of her heart turned to a whisper through her veins, she realized that all her aches faded into pleasant warmth, and the sense of bulged scars unhealed and promising to remain forever… disappeared.

"Lovely as you ever were. Lucky for you I am an old man whose flirtatious days are passed."

The flirty smile spoke otherwise, but she didn't care a wit. Her hand shot to her scalp. The skin was smooth, the hairline even, and there wasn't a hint of heat from infection. "Holy heavens."

"Indeed. Erginle smiles upon she who returns the codex of her father. No man will pity you, they'll simper at your feet. Every woman will still wish she looked like you."

Meliu blushed. *Too old to flirt, the hells.* "I've no words to thank you."

"No words are necessary for me, my child. Pray to Erginle to give thanks, and to Tulule for making her kindness possible."

The twinkle in his blue eyes made her wish he wasn't too old to flirt with, but he pulled his gold-threaded cowl over his head and strolled from her. She turned to watch him saunter away. "We will speak again, my child. Soon."

A few days later he was dead, without her having heard his voice again. She prayed then, too, and thanked his soul for the kindness he'd done for her.

Two

The Risen Lord

Be strong when your enemy believes you weak. Be fast when your enemy believes you slow. Be alive when your enemy believes you dead. All these things are true and more, but you will be most deadly when your enemy believes you a friend.

—*Codex of Sol*

One Day to the Eve of Snows

Meliu dozed in a cell a half-candle's walk from where she'd lived her days in Istinjoln. She felt she was awake, but in her mind she relived the day over and over: Dareun's soul sundered, Ulrikt rising from the dead, and his fiery declaration of war on the clans. It felt at once an unbelievable glory and a horrifying revelation. She figured she should be awed. She figured she should be terrified. Instead she was confused, numb. Even her scholar's curiosity had left her.

Or at least she tried to make it go away.

The dream residing behind her eyelids always lead to Dareun's Sundering, and from the brilliant rainbows of the Ten

Winds a Shadow fell. The thing stared at her without eyes, hating her as much as she hated it. All the while, Dareun screamed in ten discordant voices.

What does any of this have to do with Shadows? The Codex of Sol; I held the answers.

Her eyes opened every time the question and response came, and her conscious mind scuttled the enquiry. She'd held the book, and its lock defeated her, there was little point in dwelling on what it concealed.

She dozed again, and she reentered Istinjoln's courtyard on a day the sun burned white and pure. This time she kneeled alone before the sarcophagus of Ulrikt, and cast no shadow in Erginle's perfect Light. Everything was wrong, she recognized and dismissed this truth in the way of all dreamers, and when instead of Lord Priest Ulrikt rising from the dead, a serpent slunk over the rim of the golden box, her thoughts remained steady. Unconcerned. Unafraid. Unthinking.

The beast slithered closer, its body curling and unwinding, its forked tongue tasting the air, its glistening black eyes locked with her own. It grew as it approached, first as big around as a man's arm, then a leg, then the waist of a tiny girl such as herself. By the time it stopped in front of her, curling and rising into the air, the creature could've swallowed the Broldun lord priest whole.

She didn't breathe nor swallow, she just stared at the massive tongue flickering through the thin slit of its mouth. Its breath was of roses and garlic as it hissed. The tongue retracted, and the body froze as the great maw opened to reveal fangs dripping brown poison that smoked upon hitting the ground, and the air around suffered the reek of sulfur.

When the thing spoke, she was little surprised. "When the eye of the Fire Lion burns, a New Age begins."

The Fire Lion was the symbol of Sol; its eye burning seemed nothing unusual. "Into which hell have I fallen?"

The serpent's mouth closed but laughter echoed all around. Her head swiveled, lazy and unworried; Istinjoln was still empty to her eye, but someone was out there. Instinct told her it was so; a tingle on the back of her neck followed.

The snake's head ducked and rose and its mouth opened again. Black wings flapped from its jaws; a huge green-eyed raven who laughed so loud she covered her ears. From the empty sky a book dropped in her lap, and the great bird swooped towards its pages.

The *Codex of Sol.* The raven's claws ricocheted from the book's cover, wings beating her face as it ascended with an empty grip. The bird's laughter trailed into the distance, following the bird who sped beyond the eastern horizon. Not until it was a disappearing dot in the sky, did she dare to touch the tome. And it faded into nothingness.

"Into which hell have I fallen, serpent?"

"To which heaven have you risen?"

"There are no snakes in the heavens."

"And there is no Meliu in the hells."

Was this beast so sure? After all, how many Melius had lived and died before her? "If this isn't a hell, where am I?"

The voice changed into that of her father, deep and foreboding, with a gravel born of whiskey and smoke. "Within your own mind, whelp. Yer the same dumb little bitch who always thought she was so godsdamned smart."

Her heart pounded; she'd taken this man's shit for too many

years with an open mouth. Her fury built and her tongue burned to match her kin's loathing, but a voice interrupted.

"Meliu." The snake disappeared and the pound of her heart eased in an instant. The tone was gentle, smooth, so unlike her father. But she was struggling to recognize something so familiar. "Meliu."

Her eyes flitted open.

Lord Priest Ulrikt smiled as he leaned over her, a hand nudging her shoulder. "Meliu."

She must've awakened into another dream: *Ulrikt's dead. No, not dead no more. Is he real?* "My Lord Priest?" The cobwebs of sleep were thick in her brain and her tongue dry.

"Yes, my child. I apologize for waking you at such an awkward time."

"My will is yours to command." And besides, she'd crawled into her covers early, overwhelmed by the strangeness of the day.

"Good. Good. I have need of a devoted soul, and I know the priestess who brought me the *Codex of Sol* may be trusted with all things." His hand reached into his robes, and for a moment she wondered if her dream hadn't been prophecy. But he didn't hand her the *Codex*, just a scroll sealed by his own ring.

"What is it?"

He smiled, and she half expected some smart-assed quip. "It is a missive intended for High Priestess Adelin."

Meliu knew the name: Adelin headed the temple of Erginle in Choerkin Fost. She took the scroll. "You've Bearers for this job."

His grin made her feel a fool. "A Bearer draws attention, and can't talk their way out of trouble like a pretty girl." The twinkle in his eye reminded her how much a flirt the old man was. "In five days Adelin will meet you at the Burning Rock. At dawn."

Where the Choerkin executed Lord Priest Imrok of Girn.

"If you should arrive late, or she doesn't meet you that morning, open the scroll and follow its instructions. Do not fail me."

Authorized to open a scroll sealed by the lord priest was an honor more frightening than carrying the damned thing. "I won't." She sat up in bed, aware of his stare at her bare shoulder. "When do I leave?"

He stood and turned to the door. "Grab whatever you might need. Songs, extra gear, whatever is at hand. Peasant's clothes, even. A monk waits for you at the stables. He will be your escort south. Follow the main road and follow it fast. The seal on that scroll will get you fresh ponies in every village along the way. Sleep little, time is of the essence." He turned with his hand on the frame of the door. "We will speak again, my child. Soon."

He disappeared into the hall.

"The last time you said that you died."

His voice came distant, but strong and clear. "But I was not wrong, was I?"

She ducked, blushing, embarrassed that he'd heard her. She kept her next thoughts to herself: *The man has good ears and a wandering eye.*

* * *

The monk who greeted her at the stables, with two ponies saddled and ready to ride, was a fellow named Jinbin. She knew his name but scarce else. He was a couple years younger than her, and not a bad-looking man, but she took an immediate liking to him when she spotted a third pony with a travel cask of ale draping over either side.

Meliu grinned and cocked her head. "Did you steal those or are you bedding one of the brewmasters?"

"Neither! But I wasn't going to take a ride at night with some priestess without motivation." He stared at her face, holding up a lantern for a better look. "I'd heard your scalp was damned near taken off."

"We've fine healers in Istinjoln." She figured he wouldn't believe who'd healed her. "And the gods are kind so long as we hurry." She put foot to stirrup and slung herself into the saddle. Stared at the monk.

"Right." He gave the animal a hard look before crawling onto the pony's back, less familiar with riding than she was, but once settled he looked the part. "And uh, just where the hells are we going?"

She glanced to the gates, noting they were open, and heeled her gelding. "Didn't they tell you anything?"

"When High Priest Woxlin steps to my guard post and tells me there's two casks of ale on a pony waiting for me… Well, I stopped listening after that." She laughed, but the man's love for ale reminded her of another monk; her laughter faded as she pondered on Tokodin's fate. The odds of surviving a week in the mountains after a Colok attack, well, Tokodin's dice were never that lucky. Not for him at least.

They rode beneath the gates and within a flicker after they passed gears ground and iron portcullis lowered behind them. With moonlight, the road ahead was clear enough they wouldn't skid down its cliffs.

They rode in silence until Jinbin caught up and reined in beside her. "We're riding into the night and rumor speaks of the Wakened Dead to the north. Some say it's how you almost lost your face." His voice betrayed his nerves with a fidget in its tone.

She didn't know how much to say. "Yeah. The Wakened. Worse. But no worries, monk. We're headed south all the way to the Fost." She smiled, knowing the way of men enough to know she'd comfort him with this single glance. "And the quicker we get there, the quicker we get to enjoy the ale."

"A ride to the Fost. What could *possibly* go wrong?"

"Would you like a list?"

His head bobbed. "No, I don't need the particulars."

They laughed and rode, and Meliu learned much of brewing she never knew, nor cared to know, but the monk's words were a helpful distraction from darker thoughts. Wheat, barley, hops, oats, and honey. Her mind glazed over, paying little attention except to nod now and again.

They passed through the steepest foothills leading from Istinjoln and into the rolling hills beyond by the middle of the night. It was cold, their breaths puffing in front of their faces, but prayer heated their bodies and spirits. The monk had fallen silent, and the world was at peace except for the clop of hooves and the occasional hoot of an owl, or the rarer bobcat's scream.

She swayed in the saddle staring at the bright stars above when it came: A sensation like a puff of air down the back of her neck, straight through her robes, that spread chills to the tips of her toes.

There was a faint sound as if the world sighed.

The ponies nickered and skipped in their steps, prancing toward a trot or faster without reins holding them back. "Easy, sweet boy. Easy." She rubbed the pony's mane, memories of a similar pulse from the Shrine of Burdenis shredding her every sense of security. The night became darker and it terrified her to look back. But terror didn't stop her.

Beyond the horizon, where Istinjoln must sit, a beam of light rose into the sky. She followed its trail to the heavens to find a star that shouldn't be.

"When the eye of the Fire Lion burns…"

Jinbin's voice was hoarse. "Was that on your list?"

"No. But it is now." She turned in the saddle and with the barest nudge her gelding broke into a trot. Her biceps burned as she held the poor beast's energy at bay, preventing it from breaking into a cantor.

Jinbin first trailed behind, but the keg pony lurched, bucked, and drug he and his mount ahead. The casks bounced against the animal's ribs as Jinbin's left arm stretched to hold on to the rope. With his right, he clung to rein and mane to keep his ass in the saddle. "Shit! What d'you think this'll do to the ale?"

And against all reason she laughed.

THREE

Pretty Bird Flying

Let your enemy know you. Convince your enemy they know you. Reinforce that they know you. Bleed them with their mistaken knowledge of you; the moment the enemy realizes they never knew you at all, take their head in victory.

—*Codex of Sol*

Meliu wasn't unused to being horseback; a priest who trained ponies had been keen on her since she'd turned sixteen. But the freedom on the road was a sensation she'd never experienced while riding circles in the courtyard. The sun shone, and compared to the foothills, the weather was pleasant. A comfortable breeze rustled the leaves of trees in the midst of shifting to oranges and reds, and there weren't more than a handful of travelers on the road to worry her. The song of snow buntings and the twitter of pipits escorted them south as she breathed deep and took in the details of the world around her.

She'd never understood tranquility before.

The beam of light and its terror three nights ago had faded into the back of her mind. Her heart would race now and again when her wits reminded of the evil behind them, but the wonder of this peace made it impossible to hurry.

She knew she should push her pony hard; she bore a message from the Lord Priest, for Erginle's sake. *Hell's, he might be King Priest by now.* The ponies were her definitive excuse; they were riding a long stretch of rising ground in the river's bluffs, and the village of Amdan, she guessed, remained horizons away. *What good to wear out the ponies so we're afoot?*

Breathing came without the pressure of people nor the oppression of stone walls, and though they followed a road, they could change direction on a whim. Most folks would take such opportunity for granted, but after eighteen years spent in tunnels and halls, she found the open compass of choices exhilarating. She maybe understood now why the tinker loved his life of traipsing from village, to city, to monastery.

The real world shook her daydreams from her skull with the cadence of hooves in a hurry. She twisted in her saddle and the lone rider was on them in a flash, bearskin cloak flapping. It wasn't the first warden they'd seen riding hard the past couple of days, but this was the first to bother with words.

"Ride for the Fost!"

Before Meliu could muster her wits, she stared at the warden's back, the horse's lathered thighs, and a trail of dust.

"What! Why?" She feared she knew, but hoped she was wrong.

Hooves slid in the dirt and the horse spun to face them. Turned out the warden was a young woman. "Demons have swarmed Istinjoln, all I know. Ride! Or yer both deader'n a forgotten song."

"Thank you."

The girl spun and spurred, tucking her head into the horse's mane.

Jinbin eyed her. "I've a feeling you know what the hells she was talking about."

"No. Kind of. It's above your rank, monk."

"Nothing that might kill me is above my rank, I figure."

"You don't know the Church so well, then." Meliu smirked, and his face turned red with growing frustration. "They wouldn't kill you, they'd take your body and soul. And that's more than you wanted to know."

She pushed her mare into a trot and slipped into a canter. By the time they reached Amdan the ponies puffed and hung their heads, and the stables were none too thrilled to saddle new mounts so close to sundown. The scroll with Ulrikt's seal didn't deny a stablehand's right to grumble and cuss, so long as they grumbled and cussed while doing their job, so fresh ponies would be ready to ride in a flare or two.

Amdan's stables had stalls for twenty, half the population of this tiny village, she'd wager, but it held four ponies. Logs bigger around than her waist composed the frame, and red clay tiles crowned its roof. Meliu leaned against the frame of the double doors, staring down the single, lantern lit aisle with its stone floor.

Jinbin slid close and spoke so folks wouldn't overhear. "What the hells are demons who take men's souls doing in Istinjoln?"

"On Erginle's hand, I swear I don't know. The Shadows were at the Shrine of Burdenis, too. For a while now."

"You served at the Crack? Woxlin served there, rumor speaks, and half the high priests in Istinjoln too. How many scars you got?"

She groaned, it was a question she hated. "Ten more than One Lash." It was her attempt to belittle the accomplishment and shut folks up.

He whistled. "Eleven scars, honored with a post at the Crack. You were marked for the high priesthood. Don't even say you weren't, and you're telling me you don't know what's going on?"

"No. I don't."

The nature of his silence, the tilt of head and body, the curling lip, spoke to his lack of trust. Hells if she blamed him. His next words were the first to surprise her since they'd departed Istinjoln.

"Is it real?"

She flinched, any gambler's cool she possessed snapped for a flicker, and there wasn't a way he missed it. "Is what real?"

"The *Codex of Sol*." His stare burned into her eyes.

"I'm not sure what rumors you—"

"Punt rumor to the hells. A scholar at the Crack with a message from the Lord Priest, and we've all heard whispers of the library. Tales of prophecy have burnt every adherent's ears for centuries. Ulrikt rising from the dead, the Taken in Istinjoln?"

"Look…" She licked her teeth then lips, exasperated. No need for a spat with bigger battles on the horizon. "Yes. It's real. I've seen it. I've touched it. I've never opened its pages." *Not that I didn't try.* Hooves clopped down the stone-paved aisle of the stable, granting a moment's reprieve. "It's a dead subject, and not because we have company."

"I can paint the portrait."

She snarled, her voice low. "The hells you can. I've seen ugly pieces of it and I still don't have a shittin' idea what's going on. So we shut our mouths and ride, hear me?"

He raised his hands in defeat as she took a pony's reins. Leather creaked as she mounted.

Jinbin said, "We should warn these people."

Meliu grimaced but turned to the stablehand, a gray-haired monk she suspected hadn't seen Istinjoln in thirty years, except in his dreams. "You've heard there's trouble to the north?"

The man nodded with a cough, but his mouth cut a determined line across his face. "We won't be abandoning our posts without word from Istinjoln."

She understood his devotion, and without proof of what she feared in the north, she didn't push. "Be prepared for flight, you hear? I've no idea if trouble will make it this far south, but if it does you gotta be ready."

"Aye, priestess." The monk turned and strolled back into the lantern-lit hall. She heard him grumble: "Too damned old to be running anywhere."

She turned her attention back to Jinbin. "Best I can do."

Jinbin squinted at the saddle as his pony eyeballed him, groaned as he lifted a foot into the stirrup. "Gods, my ass aches and my thighs are rubbed raw."

With fresh horses and rations they moved on, walking the first couple horizons to warm the ponies into a long ride. The silence between the two lasted only a few hundred paces.

"Why you?"

"You can't clamp that hole, can you?" The sound of the monk's voice and its disrespectful tone grated her nerves, but the question was valid. "Because Lord Priest Ulrikt trusts me." She'd accepted Ulrikt's explanation, drowsy, just awakened, but the question of it being a satisfactory answer hadn't risen in her head until now.

Her words seemed to satisfy her companion, but the next question sunk a deeper chill of suspicion into her heart. "Why me? I'm a nobody."

She should've questioned this long before now; Woxlin handing him the mission should've clued her in right quick. Her brain had been on skids since the Crack. "Because you're a chunk of mud who'd do anything stupid for a couple casks of ale." Jinbin laughed, but it wasn't an answer she liked. The lord priest didn't do much by chance; hells, he acted as if he'd known all along he'd die. *Did he know?* That pinched her nerves more than any motivation surrounding the monk's presence. She squeezed her knees, and the pony broke into a trot. "We should be able to trade out ponies more often as we get closer to the Fost, we should ride hard."

"Drinking a bit of ale'd lighten the third pony's load."

More like they'd have to leave the keg pony to hurry their journey. "I've a feeling we'll need all the ale we got once we reach the Fost. We fly fast as we can. Sober."

Four

Crown and Moons

Listen, petition, sedition, what motivation?
How often your mouth moves does not make fact,
nor prove your eyes open to reality.
Telling truth is not speaking fact.
Truth is in the eye of the believer;
Fact is outside the eye of the father.
Not of my birth, but of my creation.
Not so grandiose.
Not Creator, but creator, silly bird, assured, most lured, seeing seeking truth from a single eye of dark, the lark, the bark, embark to find the stark of my creation.
Stark. Fact.
Sedition in creation's vision.

.—*Tomes of the Touched*

Meliu didn't know what to make of the lord priest's instructions: Meet High Priestess Adelin at the burning Rock at dawn. She did know time ran short.

They cut cross-country for the last couple days, not to save horizons, but to avoid the rising streams of people moving for the Fost. It was sunset, and the ponies nickered as they stood astride a hill overlooking a road leading straight to the Fost's gates. Two dozen or more people walked with beleaguered strides, several pulling carts, and they didn't look near stopping for the night.

Jinbin said, "The Black Bell's been rung."

The saying was an old one, dating to a fable from the Age of God Wars. In the High Temple of Koldesfin, it was said, hung a massive steel bell blackened by the fires of Sol. In times of invasion the bell swung, chimed, sang to the people summoning them to their capital and King Priest to defend the Holy Land. It surprised her to hear the monk speaking of such an obscure legend. "Come on."

The group of people stopped at the sound of hooves, turning to face them with pitchforks, clubs, and other make do weapons.

Meliu brandished her finest smile. "Peace, children of Sol. From where do you hail?"

The men relaxed, weapons dipping toward dirt. A man tall enough to look her in the eye as she sat astride the pony strode from the main group, in his hand a crude iron pike, a weapon often gifted to common folk who fought in some battle. Behind him, a young child broke into sobs and intermittent screams. "The village of Ledin, priestess. From where do you ride?"

It was unusual they'd question her; they were leery, and she wasn't keen on telling the truth. "Peluks. Mind if we accompany you good folk?"

"No offense to yer holiness, but we ain't looking for no strangers. Word is the troubles come from you holies, in Istinjoln."

"I was born in Veleen, not so far from Ledin. You might know my father's piss-poor cooking, if you been through there."

"The Raging Dragon?" She nodded, and his lips squirreled into a smirk. "Never knew the man's name, nor naught of any child, but his stew has a way with sticking in a man's gullet."

"Sticking and growling its way back up. You should be raised on the stuff."

"You've my sympathies fer that, still…"

"Darkness falls, and I can be useful on the road." She bowed her head in prayer. A connection to Erginle warmed the base of her skull, and she felt the soothing calm of Light spread through her bones and into every muscle. It was an unnatural peace, tranquility so powerful that the weak became addicted. *Thank you, Erginle, for this Light you give me.* She released the energy, willing it to form above the heads of the people.

A field of Light spread a hundred paces long and wide. Lesser prayers would create simple balls of Light; a girl with only eleven scars didn't bother with lesser. This Light didn't promise a mere clear view on a moonless night. The creases of their brows faded, the intensity around their lips relaxed, and their grips on weapons eased. The perfection of the Light sharpened their every cue of serenity, and Meliu sensed Erginle's will seeping into their souls. Even the sobbing child went silent.

Meliu smiled and squeezed her pony's ribs. "I understand if you don't want us with you, but you're most welcome to join us."

They rode to the lead of the villagers with a sauntering gait, and the people fell in behind.

Jinbin glanced her way several times before he broke his silence. "You're good."

Meliu smiled, letting herself enjoy the moment. "Better than most, so I've been told. If luck is our friend, the Fost won't question our arrival with these folks in tow."

The monk chortled. "Better indeed."

"Don't be too impressed, it don't do shit against Shadows or Taken."

"That's... unfortunate."

She grunted. The memory of Angin lifting her from the floor, the razor edge of a stalagmite damned near scalping her, then watching what used to be a peaceful giant of a man have his head split open by a blow to save her life, screamed through her mind's eye. She raised her arms, closed her eyes, and sucked a deep breath, letting the peace of Light wash the horrors away.

When she opened her eyes, she wasn't the terrified child from those caves any longer; she was back in control.

"It's dumber'n the hells, but I have to ask: Do Shadows cast shadows?"

Meliu rocked in her saddle, stifling a dark giggle. "No. No, they don't, now you mention it."

They traveled slow and steady with the Light soothing more than the people's spirits; it numbed the aches and pains of their bodies. They toiled without complaint as they plodded over rising hills, pulling carts as if wooden poles and planks had become part of their being.

They laid eyes on the Fost some time past midnight; the massive walls stood dotted with torches and lanterns placed so close if you squinted they blurred into a chain of fire. The Choerkin knew something was coming, but there was no way in the hells they were prepared for such evil if Shadows reached this far.

Meliu hadn't a clue what to expect upon reaching the Fost, but as they approached the western gate, she wondered if she should enter the city. Fear of Shadows and Taken consumed her mind these past few days, driving out another problem born in the hells: What if word of Ulrikt's declaration of war traveled faster than they did? Far as she knew, every adherent in the city was dead or jailed.

She released the power of prayer and they rode to the gate by the light of the stars. The portcullis ground open as they approached, men with lanterns stepping from the maws of the city, and her unease grew. They glanced twice at Jinbin and his robes, but held deathly stares for her. Some of those men on the walls had arrows nocked; she'd be a corpse in a flicker if they decided she was an enemy.

A guardsman stepped from the gate to stand in front of her, a halberd in his grip, but not so close to block arrows from above. "What's your business, priestess?"

"This good monk and I served in Peluks, and on meeting these fine folks they served us strange tidings. So we joined them. Do the devout now need a reason to visit the Temple of Erginle?"

"Strange tidings?" He spat, and his words escaped with a snarl. "Demons in Istinjoln, and assassins striking the Choerkin? Tell me what questions I shouldn't ask at this hour?"

Meliu's blood chilled. The villagers had passed through the gates, leaving her and Jinbin alone. A prayer for Light would ease her nerves, but could also get her killed. "Assassins? I pray no lives were lost."

"Your prayers are too late. Knives in the night, upon the Eve of Snows."

"On the Eve of Snows? Them folks said the troubles in Istinjoln started then."

"No holies are to pass the gates, in nor out, after dark. Hells welcome coincidences; mortals question them."

The quote was closer to *hells embrace coincidence, while mortals question them, but they're created by the gods,* and in full context spoke of fate, but she took his point. Lying to this man would be a fool's play, even if she could conceal her doubts. "Your suspicions are… understood. But if I return by light of day?"

"If you'll forgive a search, we'll allow entrance to the temple."

"And my man? Might I send him onward tonight? I'm sure he'd share a few mugs of ale for your trouble."

The guardsman scratched behind his ear. "Might be, so long as we give escort to the temple doors. If they don't open for him, his ass is back out here minus the ale."

"I could spare a few pints." Jinbin turned to her with a glower. "Those doors better open, or you owe me."

"You get to sleep inside for the night, you owe me."

"If you think a feather tick puts you to the advantage, you're crazier than a four-eyed bat."

"Just do as told, monk." It came out harsher than she intended, but her pang of guilt was mild as he'd lacked proper manners the entire journey.

"Yes, my priestess." It shocked her his tone didn't hold a peevish note.

Meliu reined her pony to the northern edge of the road, watching as Jinbin and the guards disappeared.

No doubt the monk would be content within those walls, where he wouldn't even have to tap his kegs to get drunk, but even without the added threats of recent days, something about cities gave her the shivers. Veleen had been full of filth and fights, but was more open streets than bustle. Istinjoln housed a couple thousand adherents and guards, but most times you could feel alone if you liked. Lay folk crammed the avenues of the Fost, she'd heard, all of them smelling more of fish and goat than human. And now, after a couple years living in isolation at the Crack, she couldn't imagine a place more alien to her than a city.

Riding in the wilderness with no crowds and no caves, she found she had an affinity for this life; open sky and voiceless breezes were welcome even if chill.

Knees squeezed, and the pony moseyed northwest as her mind ran circles. She wished she knew what had happened in Istinjoln on the Eve of Snows. She wished she knew what prophecy in the Codex sought its fruition. She wished she knew how many of these people might soon kill others, Taken. *No, Istinjoln won't allow the Shadows to reach so far south.* But then, why were people so far south already fleeing?

A prayer for Light steadied her breaths and ushered the troubling thoughts from her head. She held the energy tight as a babe with a blanket, leaving the night dark, but her soul brightened.

She guided the pony from the road, maybe a horizon from the Fost, before finding a spot that suited her fancy. She left the pony tacked, gave him water from her canteen, and sat with her back to a small tree as the animal grazed.

She determined she wouldn't sleep, but as time passed her lids slipped. She must've dreamed she stayed awake, for the dawn was on her in what felt a moment.

She stirred and leaped to her feet, startling the pony, for a flicker only, before it returned to grazing. After a cold breakfast of jerked turkey, bread, and water, she tacked up and mounted, determined to finish her mission.

The Burning Rock was a reviled legend in Istinjoln, akin to the *Codex of Sol* to the Choerkin, she figured. It was easy to find, her and the pony might've damned near stumbled into it the night before, and her first impression was underwhelming.

A boulder. Blackened by fire. A hole in the top. The only thing to give her pause were the famous words carved in its face:

In Fire may loyalty be reborn.

The notion of Lord Priest Girn burning into a charred log at this very spot didn't phase her near so much as she expected.

The notion she might burn here next gave an instant of chill with tightened throat.

Jitters shook their way through her body as she sat the saddle, waiting. Ulrikt had declared holy war on the Choerkin, all the clans, for that matter. What sense did it make sitting a hundred paces from their gates? Worse, if Istinjoln had sent assassins. Was the pulse, were the Shadows part of the war? She tried to discard this notion, but it stuck to her like a trail of spit.

She dismounted, strolled around the stone, aiming to loosen her muscles and relax. But her nerves stayed on edge. For a while. Then she grew bored. The morning's rays headed towards a midday sun, and the casual glances of guards turned to curious stares.

No high priest in sight. Open the scroll, that's what Ulrikt had commanded if Adelin didn't meet her.

She put foot to stirrup and swung into the saddle, turning west so as the guards couldn't see. The scroll shook from her sleeve and she stared at its seal, her heart beating an uncomfortable rhythm. She cracked the holy seal, terrified what Church secrets she might find, but what she read clutched her lungs.

She read her own name, and the only two words which followed:

Flee Kaludor.

* * *

It didn't take a search to find Jinbin; he lay stretched out on a bed in the temple's guest quarters (both kegs nearby, although from the smell of him she guessed one was lighter than before) snoring with the rasp of a two-man saw.

She rapped the middle of his forehead with a knuckle. "Wake up monk, it's the middle of the shittin' day."

The only thing that moved was his eyelids. "Gods woman… priestess, have mercy on a man's head, would ya?"

She stretched the scroll open and held it in front of his face; close enough she was certain his head pounded with the strain to focus.

"What the hells is that?"

"This… This is the message the lord priest gave me to deliver to a high priestess. No one showed up."

He sat up, glanced at her. "You aren't a high priestess."

"Monk, you're a genius. How'd you fail the priesthood again?"

"I failed 'cause I took to the whip like I did drink." He rubbed his forehead. "You're so smart… So what the hells does this mean, eh?"

"Means we need to find a boat." Ramifications, implications, they'd have to wait for another time. "Why" was a powerful and unseemly word right that moment.

"I'm wagerin' there's a couple thousand souls out there with that idea already. You got songs to buy out berths?"

Close to a thousand songs packed a small pouch hidden in her robes, but it'd only be a fortune to a fisher. She never figured saving her coins would mean much. Rowing, or a single sail to… where? *Herald's Watch. Damned to hells. More Choerkins.* "We've little choice." She eyeballed his kegs of ale, grinned.

His head lolled. "Oh no."

"If it comes down to your life or your ale?"

"I'm sure they're one and the same."

"I'd think your hangover'd make that decision easy." His stare irked her. "I ain't got time for this jabber, flicker you see a

Shadow you'll be throwing that ale at the first seaman you see. I'll head for the docks, troll some offers, see what can be had."

She turned and stomped through the open arch, wishing there was a door to slam for emphasis. She rushed past adherents without the formality of bows or even nods and didn't give a damn if it offended them.

She opened the temple's main door, and a rock sailed past her head the moment she stepped into the street. She ducked late as the stone clattered against the wall, and a man typical as any screamed at her, untypical fury in his eyes. "You priests have brought the hells upon us!"

Monks who guarded the gates to the temple stepped between her and the layman. She took a breath and strode from safety, pulling her cowl from her face in the hopes a pretty young face would attract fewer stones than a dark hood. Once away from the temple fewer hostile eyes glared her way, and by the time she reached the wharf folks no longer bothered to look at her at all.

There were more people than planks on the docks, and maybe enough quality ships to haul half of them. If Istinjoln hadn't held, the butchery on its way to these streets tied her gut in knots. And Ulrikt's message boded ill, suggesting Istinjoln would fall, or was never meant to hold. Celestial Gates were monstrosities from the Age of God Wars… Oh, she'd heard the rumors while serving in the Chanting Caverns, but she put no more weight to them than any words she might imagine in the mountain winds singing down the tunnels.

She should've paid more attention.

She wandered past boats filled with men and women who stank of fish and sweat, her mind scratching at memories to dig up a bone, even as she dismissed seeking passage on one of these tubs that looked like they'd turn over from bumping a tortoise. When she stopped staring low and gazed to the sky, her feet stopped. A blue flag snapped in the distance, with the eight phases of the moon, in white, surrounding a crown.

The word slipped between her lips: "Luxuns." She'd worn their perfumes and their silks, both luxuries she regretted now she could use the songs, but only in her fanciest dreams had she considered ever meeting one.

There was no way she'd get on that ship, the finest to sail the seas, folks said. Still, her feet carried her that direction. Her Pa always said, if you want the best you can get, aim the highest and work your way down. Were Luxuns attracted to humans? No, even if she offered to spread her legs, which she wouldn't… Or would she? *Taken or taken, one I'd survive. What won't I do to keep breathing?* She snorted the notion away.

She needed a plan; her mind was a tally tablet scrubbed clean. So when she came to face her destination, instead of being filled with genius and inspiration, she stood and stared.

Meliu didn't know a sheep's bleat about sailing ships, but the Luxun vessel was beautiful. Three masts rose high, with a crow's nest atop the middle, and each was painted in tasteful pastels: blues, reds, and greens. Each ring was maybe the height of a man and marked by a broad brass collar. The colors grew lighter as they rose toward the sky. It wasn't a mere ship; it was a floating piece of art. And it looked fast. Sturdy. The former a quality she figured most of these floating hells lacked.

Look like you belong, and you do. She smiled and winked her way past a trio of Silone guards with a confident gait to her step. They smiled and gave her a nod without a question. Easy as a whistle, but she slowed her steps to think.

The Luxuns were an unrivaled seafaring power, if she could trust the stories, yet folks knew little of them. Her eyes twitched as the memory struck, a single word in a trade ledger which meant something akin to "permission to board." She hoped the merchant who made the note knew hells from heavens when he'd scrawled that note, or she might end up cussing at the captain.

It wasn't difficult to discern the Luxun who appeared to be in charge: She stood tall, the feathers on her head raised as exotic birds Meliu'd seen sketched in foreign tomes. She eyeballed sailors and shouted commands, but she wasn't the captain. A statue of a man, eyes hard and unflinching, his hands twined behind his back, that's who she needed.

She cleared her throat and projected her voice and will. "*Nonfoñu.*"

The Luxun's eyes twitched her way before he tucked his head and meandered toward her with a grin. "*Nonfoñu. Erbit entoñeo.*" The guards stepped aside, their spears uncrossing to permit her passage. A dozen hesitant steps across the gangplank brought her to stand on a ship for the first time.

She gifted the man she assumed the captain with a broad, sardonic smile she'd practiced for hours staring into a mirror. Most often she used it when insulting someone when she wanted them to take it for a joke. "*Nonfoñu* is all you're going to get, but I'd love the chance to learn more of your speech."

He clucked his tongue, and it sounded nothing like a chicken; she tried not to smirk. "A priestess of words. We don't hire to… what is it you say? Tutor?"

"My name is Meliu of Veleen, I need passage to the Watch, I can pick up some language along the way."

"In two days?"

"In two days."

"Can you sail?"

She couldn't but giggle at herself. "I haven't spent a flicker on the water in my life. Captain?"

"Captain Intœño." He stepped back, clicking his heels with a bow. "But, what good would you be to this vessel? Peoples from around the world serve on Luxun ships, but they must be of a purpose."

"I can save you all, there's an evil coming."

"Oh. Mmm." His bland grin betrayed nothing of surprise nor fear; his dismissal scrunched her lips. "We have heard the talk on the docks."

"But you haven't seen it, I have. You need to sail."

"You are a peculiar and entertaining girl, and I like you because I can see your eyes without straining my neck. You are a runt amid your people."

It was a comment she'd heard a thousand times, but never from someone of her own height. "To the Silone, the whole of your people are runts. With peculiar hair."

The feathers on his head stood, beautiful blues and greens reflecting in the black as the sun struck them, then he guffawed. "What price can you pay?"

"Three hundred Songs." His lips turned a darker blue when pursed. "And two travel kegs of Istinjoln ale. The hells if that isn't a deal for a short trip."

His feathers fluffed and relaxed. "Passage is yours for one keg, but it's by our schedule."

"We need to leave now—"

"Impossible. The *Entiyu Emoño* is under contract. We do not leave without the lady."

"Death is coming. No lie."

"And I believe you, but we must meet this death before we sail without the lady."

She snorted, frustrated. Difficult as crawling from the hells to convince people of danger. "She must be rich. Is her gold worth your life?"

His lips flipped into a pouting frown. "While I well know the lady could afford whatever price I set, no. I owe her a debt."

Well, that's the shits. The Luxuns were known for their love of gold, and she might outbid a price, but she'd never match the value of an honorable debt. She measured her next words before speaking. "Honor trumps gold, even if only by a little."

Intœño's smile returned. "In truth."

"Who is this lady?"

He tapped his nose, but she didn't understand what the gesture meant. "You are a bold one."

"Shouldn't I know with whom I travel?"

"Fair." He cocked his head for a flicker, clucked once. "One of your northern brethren."

The smirk which followed suggested he didn't care if she knew he played her. And no way to question a captain's word when begging passage. "I accept your generous offer. My man and I will bring payment soon."

"Sooner is good, we remain and sail at the whim of the lady."

Meliu nodded, but a sailor passing behind the captain captured her attention. His skin was black as onyx, and his waist length hair was braided and dyed in red, green, blue, and gold. "That man… From the Trade Cities of Emerdeesh?"

The captain's brows rose as he glanced back. "No, he is Dara, from a cluster of small islands called the Olfin."

The names were none she'd ever heard. "Dara, his name or his people's?"

"He is called Uumboyo. As I said, we bring aboard great sailors from the worldwide." He tapped his nose twice. "But, you are well traveled or well read. The Dara and the Emustobo, the people of the Trade Cities, worship the Four Queens. They have more in common than not."

The Four Queens was a religion she'd read only a paragraph or two about in all her studies. All she recalled was that they believed a dreaming god created the world. "I am out of my depths with you, sir, and your knowledge of foreign peoples."

"When you've seen as many seas as my eyes, you learn things. Such as the language of giants on a frozen island." He smiled with a polite nod. "Bring your man and keg, then we will speak more."

Meliu bowed and strode back to the dock, trot-walking east to see if she might find a quicker road to the temple. The streets on this side of the city bore more pocked holes and loose bricks, but they were less crowded. Maybe because of the stench of a tannery nearby.

She took a satisfied breath and dared a legitimate smile meant for no one but herself. Way she figured, she'd done good.

"Choerkin at the gates!" A chime sounded and to the east her ears made out the grind of a portcullis.

She glanced toward the temple, just now visible to the north, but curiosity had seized her soul. She trotted down the street until she found a view of the East Gate. The portcullis stopped, and the dark of the arched entry illuminated as doors opened.

Five bedraggled riders road into the city, their horses flagged. She gasped with recognition, even if she didn't know all their names. One Lash and Ivin Choerkin, the Rat, plus a man and woman she'd seen the day of Ulrikt's rising. *Blood in the Forge, this can't be good.*

A sixth rider trailed in priest's robes, but she recognized the face soon as he looked up. *Holy Heavens! Tokodin.* "He is alive."

The urge to run to him, to hug her old friend, tickled her fancy, but as the gates swung shut and portcullis descended, the Forges defeated the Heavens. In her mind she heard Tokodin's words from that day beside the Crack of Burdenis: *The hells are coming.*

And she knew it was true.

The time for reunions would wait for another day.

What she needed was a pony, a keg, and another stupid monk to get her off this Shadow cursed island.

FIVE

Sisterly Love

Spin the wheel, feel the spiel;
will misstated lies find truth?
Are truths unspoken lies?
With how many wings does the Craven Raven fail to fly?
For how many years must a man be dead to die?

—*Tomes of the Touched*

The pitch of the scream was inhuman and seized every nerve in Meliu's body. Her muscles refused to move, and for a flicker it felt time had stopped.

Then the voice came. "What the Forges was that?"

She blinked as a deer shaking off the stare of a starving wolf, and all her blood pumped at once. Her heart beat to explode. The pony stood nearby loaded with ale. Jinbin's smile was one of terror.

"No time. There's no time. Get to the Luxun ship, swift as a falcon."

"What the hells was that noise?"

The urge to slap him brought a twitch to her fingers. "A Shadow. They're here. Now go! Go!"

He took the pony's lead, hands shaking. She'd taken two steps toward the temple before the question came. "Where the hells are you going?"

"High Priestess Adelin. They need warned. I thought I had time."

If Jinbin replied she never heard his words. She fled the stables and as she hit the middle of the courtyard a second demonic scream echoed through the city; it was distant, and she didn't bother to look. She slammed past temple guards at a full sprint, but they paid her no mind, their eyes locked somewhere behind her.

Adherents scurried through the temple's halls, hustling without running. Meliu grabbed a priest by his arm and spun him to face her. He was a big man and wrinkled by years, a priest already by the time she'd been a bare foot postulant. He deserved more respect than she gave. "Where the godsdamn is Adelin?"

Another time he might have struck her for speaking such, but on this day he answered before wrenching his arm free. "The Theater of Sol."

"Where?"

"Straight ahead and climb the horseshoe stair, central arch and you're there."

She nodded and ran, not wasting her breath on a thank you. Her sprint down a granite hall ended as doors opened into a broad room, its ceiling held aloft by a dozen ornate pillars. Stairs carved with vines and trees stood to either side of the room, leading to a balcony. She took the right stair and by the time she reached the top her lungs gasped. She took the central arch, and as promised, found High Priestess Adelin.

Meliu had met the woman several times over the years. She'd aged since last they'd met, her ruddy brown hair showing strings of silver, but there was no mistaking her.

"High Priestess…"

But she wasn't alone. High Priestess Sedut stood by her side; the women were still as two brooding hens as they stared at her.

Meliu swallowed a rock. "The Shadows, they're here. But you knew that." Meliu addressed Adelin, but her eyes couldn't escape Sedut's tranquil gaze.

"Meliu?" said Adelin. "What are you doing here, child?"

"I thought I was here to warn you. To make sure you flee Kaludor."

Adelin smiled, awkward for a priestess so stern. "We will not flee. We will fight the Shadows and lead our people to the sea."

Sedut said, "It is you who should've fled. Your prayers are worthless here."

True words, but it was their honesty that wrenched her gut. Her voice came soft. "I will." Then she gathered her courage, straightening to stand as tall as nature allowed. "Do we fight the Shadows, or do they fight for Ulrikt?"

Sedut took a step toward her, but Adelin's hand on her shoulder stopped the scornful gaze from gliding closer.

Adelin said, "Your suspicions are misplaced, and forgivable considering your experiences in the north."

"What the hells do you know about my experiences? To hells with that, what about dead Choerkin?"

"The clan has many enemies. Would the Church stoop so low to knives? May as well use poison."

Her smile wasn't out of place now, Meliu thought it sadistic. Treading further was walking on crackled ice.

Meliu nodded and shrugged her shoulders. "You fight, you lead, I guess. I'll sail for the Watch."

Sedut said, "I wish you fortunate journeys."

Meliu bowed. "To the both of you, as well."

She turned and strode for the exit, but Adelin's voice halted her for a flicker. "Meliu. Never doubt Lord Priest Ulrikt."

Meliu tucked her head and walked fast. "Never doubt," she muttered, but spoke no further in case someone listened. *Not sure I trust myself anymore, let alone that bastard.* But she'd said not to doubt him, it was Meliu's interpretation to insert trust in him. *Are those truly the same? Maybe not. Why the hells am I quibbling over a word? Because it's what you do, fool.*

She snorted at herself as she reached the bottom of the stairs. There wasn't a soul in sight, which set off her nerves and erased the semantic debate from her head. With lungs recovered she bolted for the temple's front doors and burst into the walled courtyard.

Empty.

The guards were gone, and not a single adherent stood in view, but she heard screams and shouts from Lantern Street beyond the walls. She took a couple rushed breaths then bee-lined to the gate. People streamed by as chaotic as trout battling their way up a waterfall, making her wish she were a bear to knock a few from her path.

She slipped into the flow, thankful the docks stood not so far from the temple, but once in the thick of the human swarm she couldn't see where she went without hopping for a view. "Shittin' me? Godsdamned shittin' me?" Her direction was at the mercy of the mob. "Burn the bellows!" An oaf-footed man clipped her heel, and she fell, rolling and bouncing to her feet to keep from a trampling: "Molten Forge be damned!" By the time they reached the wharfs she scraped the barrel of curses. "By the Dancing Bastards! Just let me through!"

She could see the crown and moon banner of the Luxun ship over the heads of the dolts in front of her. So far away she needed wings. Luxun honor wouldn't demand they die waiting for their patron; she needed to hurry. She squeezed sideways toward a wall and spotted a cart. Weeping children huddled beneath its boards clutching their knees to chests, but there wasn't a damned thing she could do for them or anyone else. Didn't seem she could do nothing for herself, but a desperate plan formed when she spotted urchins atop the buildings.

She climbed into the cart. The drainpipe lay in the street, but a gutter remained. *Three steps and jump. Three steps and jump.* One, two, the cart teetered on three and the valiant leap she imagined instead sent her careening into the crowd.

She bounced off a giant man's back.

Struck the cobbles.

Curled into a ball as boots kicked at her ribs and head. Curses flew at her soul from a half dozen voices.

She screamed and prayed; the Light came intense, and she unleashed its power in a blinding flash, her own eyes squeezed tight and covered by her hands.

Screams and more curses, but the blows stopped. She rose to a crouch and ran, hands still covering her face and ears, bouncing off a score of people before tumbling into open ground between two guardsman whose pikes pointed at the shouting mob. A third guard's sword leveled at her eyes.

"I've passage paid on the *Entiyu Emoño*! I must get there, I've a message for Kotin Choerkin!" She held forth Ulrikt's scroll, praying the man wouldn't take time to check her story.

His sword rose. "Go!"

Meliu scrambled to her feet and ran. Laymen crowded the

docks, but they weren't as thick with desperate folk as the streets leading here. A chill swept her spine; a flicker later an energy surged behind her. She didn't want to look, and cursed herself for a simpleton as her head turned.

Broken bodies tumbled through the air, and the head of a gigantic Shadow appeared over the throngs. Guards didn't or wouldn't hold the tide of terrified at bay. Hundreds of people roared toward her and the docks. People fell and were trampled, and she'd be next if she remained in their path. She sprinted for the ship, diving, dodging, and shoving. Her heart cried out but her lips were silent as she realized the *Entiyu Emoño* was drifting from the docks, its deck filled with people.

Folks were jumping, a woman thudded from the hull to splash into the bay, but they didn't have her running start. She would make it, she had to. She didn't survive the Crack twice to die here and now. Four more strides and leap.

Ivin Choerkin.

He stood by the rail, helping those who reached him. His face stymied her stride, and she stumbled, slid to a stop grasping a man's shoulder. *Would he shove me into the bay?* The question was moot in flickers; the jump was too far now, all she could do was stand and stare as others tried and failed at the leap. *He never even saw me.* And there stood One Lash, and Jinbin.

Hope deflated from her body with her breath. It was her ship, not theirs. She'd negotiated passage. Self-pity turned to terror when her gaze swiveled back to the city. The great Shadow plowed through human soil in a trough of broken bodies, and Taken leaped into the masses. Abandoning hope, some folks jumped into the frozen waters while the desperate shoved others. Standing at the edge, it would be her turn for a swim soon.

Meliu took her coin pouch in hand, kicked her boots off, then stripped her robes over her head and stuffed them in her pack. Her silken smallclothes, which had cost her so many songs, were all she wore when she dove.

She prayed for Heat before hitting the bay but the answer from the gods wasn't enough to save her from the pangs of crashing into icy waves. Her breath fled her lungs as she went under, and it took all her will and strength to cling to her pack and flail to the surface. Gasping, spitting, taking in more water to spit and gasp again. Heat seeped through her veins and with it strength. She'd never learned to swim more than to paddle and keep her nose above water, and that was hard as all the hells with waves risen by the rain of people tumbling into the bay.

A hand grasped her shoulder with fingers stiff and turning blue. Meliu stared as the woman submerged, thankful this stranger's fingers were too stiff to take her with her, but the meager heat of her prayer would only keep her afloat so long.

A shrill scream from the dock and she dared look up; the great Shadow stood above her, and she swore it glanced her way, and that she felt its mouthless smile. The jarring sensation of its gaze kicked her arms and legs into furious motion, a final, desperate will to survive.

Sol, I have failed you, but I beseech you don't fail me.

The warmth arrived first in her chest then spread as never before. An intensity greater than when as a child she'd grabbed a hot pan, but somehow this Heat didn't burn. It brought not only comfort, but power and determination. She looped her pack over her shoulder and stroked the water as she'd seen others do in the past. Her outreached hands struck the water and steam rose where they met.

She raised her head and spotted the shore beneath the wharf. And a flailing child a few paces away. With a confidence born of the Fires of Sol, she swam, grabbing the boy, and dragging him to the promontory with her.

She heaved her pack to shore, then drug the boy with her onto cold stone. He was alive in the clutch of her steaming arms, but unconscious, and she wrapped herself around him as best she could, willing the Heat of prayer to thaw the child's body.

A few flares later the child breathed easy, and her body no longer steamed, but not from a lack of warmth. Her skin, even her hair and silks, were dry. Sol had favored her prayer with a strength she'd never imagined. Would he provide her with a power to battle the Shadows and Taken still killing in the streets above?

She sat in relative comfort and safety, rocking a boy of maybe six years, but every sound traveling through the planks which blocked the sky were of horror. When she raised her eyes to the dock she'd escaped, she saw the giant Shadow who broke instead of taking. The thing stood at the end of the pier, arms outstretched. A hundred Taken swarmed behind its black mass.

"What the hells are you conjuring?" she muttered to herself. She glanced to the boy in her arms, her own near nakedness, and pulled her robes from her pack. They were soaked. She eased the boy from her lap, pillowing his head on her pack, and slipped into clinging wet wool. Staring at her bare feet brought choice words to mind; her socks must've slipped off in the swim.

A peculiar lull in screams from above, then the crackle and thunder of lightning. *Prayer*. Men shouted commands, and desperate, helpless cries turned to pleas for help. *Priests and Choerkin. Sedut may not have lied after all.* The great Shadow ignored whatever force was behind it, and the Taken turned in unison to stare back to the island. A grotesquery of breathing statues, many mutilated and oozing black blood. It was the first time she noticed the Taken breathed; another difference from most Wakened Dead.

Meliu stood and lifted the boy, taking him higher on the rocks. He was too much to carry far, but she needed to see what battle brought above. "I'll be back, child." She shoved her songs into her robe but left him her pack to rest his head, then hop-walked with ginger steps across the stone. A sliced foot or a turned ankle would push the boundaries of her creative curses.

There wasn't a dry way out of this place, so she hiked her robes and stepped into shallow waters. Steam rose from her feet as they slipped and slid on slippery rocks, but she kept her balance until she reached a piling with a crisscross of boards she climbed as an awkward ladder. Her head poked above the dock to find people huddled as recalcitrant lemmings, and she doubted a one noticed her squirming up the edge and hoisting her feet to the dock by a rope thick as her arm.

She didn't blame them, their attention was rapt in the battle for their lives.

Fire, lightning, smoke. Spears, arrows, javelins. Boards, stones, bottles. Whether priest, Choerkin, or commoner, everyone did their damnedest to kill and survive, and Meliu watched in distant, disconnected awe. Many of these folks in the front lines were simple people, but when faced with death, instead of blinking they grabbed whatever the hells was nearby. Men, women, young and old. *Do I possess the will and courage to fight, or just enough to sneak and survive?*

An arrow struck a Taken in the forehead, and black blood erupted from the wound; it fell from the dock, landing amidst bobbing bodies. The Shadow escaped its host, but shrieked with a sanity shirking wail. Waves struck, and the demon dissipated, leaving only an echo as a reminder of its evil.

Water. Pound my brain in the Forges… Water.

She ran through the gathered masses into emptier streets. Horrific screams from above, and her eyes raised in time to see a roof urchin's arm ripped from their body, and a Taken eyeing a pack of children.

A barrel for collecting rainwater stood on the edge of the roof, a sliver of hope if only they knew the creature's weakness.

Meliu bolted through the building's broken doors and ran up the foyer's stairs, bursting onto the roof in time to see a small girl streak toward her. But the Taken moved faster, snatching the girl's arm. Meliu lowered her shoulder and bowled straight into the monster's ribs. She caromed straight for the barrel and nearby bucket, diving for its handle. With a quick bounce to her feet, she dunked the bucket.

The Taken grasped the girl by her ankles, holding her high to split her like a wishbone. The child screamed, Meliu screamed, and at a dead sprint she heaved water at the thing.

The Taken dropped the child in an instant, wailing. Meliu grabbed the girl and pulled her away from the thing. Six children clustered around her, and they all stared as the monster slapped at its face and arms, howling in anguish.

But the godsdamned thing wasn't dying.

"The stairs! Run!" The little girl limped and Meliu lifted her to a shoulder until outside. "You can run?" The girl nodded, and they ran as fast as they could, taking a narrow street southwest toward the docks and the fighting. She glanced back; the Taken man loped on all fours behind them.

The group rounded one corner, then a second, and damned near ran down the points of spears. They screamed and ducked, the men raising their weapons to let them in the perimeter. The Taken didn't slow for a flicker and leaped, its body sliding down the length of a pike with a wail before striking the crossbar.

The warrior dropped his weapon, and swords flashed, slicing the body into chunks they kicked aside. The gore was horrific even if black-blooded rather than red, but the tendrils of Shadow creeping from the carcass suggested their reasoning.

She cast her eyes along the street, spotted another rain barrel, and ran to fill her bucket. Warriors stared at her as she stood panting over the scattered remains and the wisps of Shadow stretched thin between pieces of muscle and bone. A quick prayer passed from her lips and she tipped the bucket to pour over exposed Shadow.

Water streaked, tore, and washed away Shadow, and the thing's shriek was shrill, feeling as if it passed from this world into another along with this demon. In moments all that remained was the mutilation of what once might've been a good man.

The guards stared at her, even as she found it difficult to look away from the dead's one good eye. Her arms and shoulders shuddered. "Peace, child of Sol. Move for the Living Stars and find your way." She had no idea if the soul had passed on when Taken or not, but a prayer for the dead never felt as wasted breath.

"The Shadow. It's gone?"

Meliu ripped her eyes from the dead stare, looking up at the burly warrior. "No need to chop them to chunks. Kill the Taken, and douse the Shadow in water."

The warrior's smile was born in relief, she could see him breathe a little easier. He shouted to pikemen and archers around him: "Word down the line! Let it rain on these godsdamned bastards!" Men bellowed and cheered, and the guard turned back to her. "My thanks."

"I hope it helps." She smiled and took a step to leave, but the girl clung to her left thigh, anchoring her foot to cobble. "Let go, child. You're safe." But the girl was having nothing to do with that idea.

"First leech I've seen with two legs." The warrior laughed, and Meliu couldn't resist a grin to lighten the dark all around.

"Where's your family?"

"I don't have none."

Meliu's head rolled to blame the sky. "Then let go my leg and follow me, for the love of Januel." The girl nodded, but kept a grip on her robes with one hand; it was enough to let her walk. To the south on the docks battle raged, but on the northern perimeter commoners huddled in various states of despair and shock. Tears and rage, hugging and pounding chests, screaming at the clouds.

We need to find a boat. Her eyes squinted in disgust. *We?* She glanced to the girl at her hip. *How'd it become 'we' so fast? Shit! The boy under the dock. We'll get him safe, I swear it.* Children were never a part of her life, not even when she was one. Now she knew why. "What's your name, child?"

"Deelee."

"Well, Deelee… You don't happen to have a boat hidden around here?"

"No." The child took her dead serious. Maybe she was, in a wishful way.

"Then we need to find one, right?" A child would just make it more a pain in the ass to find a ride. Or… "Are you a good liar? I mean real good?"

"Mmhmm, yes ma'am. I can cry too, just jam my nails into my hand."

Meliu's brow arched. "I don't have no family I call my own these days neither. You're my li'l sis now, you hear?"

The child cocked her head and damned if there wasn't a tear. And the girl's hands weren't balled into fists. "I'd like that."

"So, sis, where do I find new boots?"

Six

Swarming Maggots

To ally with one enemy to destroy another is an ages old strategy to survive. With victory at hand, or even before, one must decide if this new friend is as a wolf domesticated, or if its blood still boils with the wild. Be prepared to put an arrow into your new friend's, and old enemy's, heart, lest he eat your soul.

— *Codex of Sol*

Meliu wiggled her toes in oversized boots. They weren't the fanciest boots she'd ever owned, that distinction belonged to a pair which lay lost in the Chanting Caverns. Tooled leather softer than a bunny's butt (as her mother would have said), light as sandals, and imported from the Gorotan, they'd cost five hundred songs. The price felt fair at the time, but right now she'd trade them for an hour's deep sleep.

Her new boots weren't pretty nor light, but they were sealskin and Deelee swore up and down she'd be able to run into the surf and stay dry and warm. When ugly, heavy, and an imperfect fit could save your life, they became beautiful. More beautiful if she wasn't glancing at the doors and windows, flinching every time someone passed and cast a shadow. It was only time that stood between horror and these few moments of peace.

The cobbler's shop sat on the outskirts of the perimeter set by Choerkin spears, and folks had picked over the shelves, but they both had new boots.

"Are we stealing?"

"Hard to say if the cobbler's dead or no, can't steal from the dead can you?" The girl's quizzical stare annoyed her, but touched a soft spot. "What kind of orphaned urchin are you?"

"I'm your sister now, and I never liked taking stuff, no how."

"I suppose even a young girl can be right once in a Heaven's Age. I'll leave a few coins… maybe not what these fine boots're worth, but better than nothing… if you know where we can grab clean new dresses."

Meliu picked out two dresses for each of them, heavy fur-lined cloaks, and a haversack, plus she paid for them proper; the owners of the general store weren't dead, nor had they run away. They were, however, shocked to find anyone looking to buy anything, let alone a priestess wanting something other than robes.

It was the first time in two years she'd worn anything other than her habit. At least on the outside. The new linen dress bore quality hand stitching, and they befitted the silk smallclothes underneath. When staring at the pretty girl in the mirror, she wondered if she hadn't been born to the wrong parents: The dress suited her, and she imagined she should've been born to wealthy merchants, not a violent bastard without a sense of taste and a woman who loved whiskey more than her own blood.

They stepped from the shop as new people; they weren't

a priestess from Istinjoln and a roof rat, they were two sisters wronged by an ill fate and desperate for a boat to Herald's Watch.

A Shadow's shriek jarred her senses. How quick could she slip into normality? Normal was dead, yet even a couple wicks of banter and peace had eased her wits into a vulnerable state.

Meliu clenched her jaw and narrowed her eyes, staring hard at the world around her. *Unaware makes the mightiest warrior a corpse. A child two steps ahead will never die. Try to be six steps ahead to assure those two steps are real.* Wisdom to stay alive by from the *Book of Dolomi.*

An hour earlier the wharf had been a roaring mass fighting for survival, now there was a frightening quiet over the area. With Deelee's hand in hers, she sought the nearest guardsman. "Sir? Pray, what has happened? Were the Shadows defeated?"

"Way I hear, no. There's a standoff at the docks. And still plenty of Taken roaming the Fost." Which explained why his eyes never left the streets behind them.

Meliu nodded and bowed her head as she walked away. A standoff was better than slaughter, but what sense did it make?

"These monsters, we're winning?"

"No, child. But we ain't dead neither."

High Priestess Adelin never promised victory, but leading the people to the sea. Harsh reality, defeatism, or all a spoke in the War Wheel? "Come, Deelee, let's see if we can find Auntie."

Meliu needed to see about the boy and a boat, but her gut compelled her to spy on the battle first. They wriggled between common folk, and claimed a search for their mother whenever they stepped on toes, until they reached a stretch of street with a view from higher than the docks. They were too far away for details, but a quick prayer allowed her eyes to cut the distance in half.

There was a standoff of a sorts, just as the guard had said. A wall of fog or smoke, or maybe gauzy shadow, rose between men and Taken. The barrier horseshoed into the bay, so any access would need come straight at the end of the dock where the great Shadow stood. Silone warriors paced its boundary on land, but the Taken sat in precise rows stretching down the dock, legs folded and hands resting in their laps as if in meditation. The scene was surreal when compared to the manic bloodthirst she'd always seen. The great Shadow stood just as she'd left it, arms outstretched and staring out to the bay.

"What the hells?" She stared for a wick stupefied, before her wits snapped to a nameless book which dated from the Age of Warlords: *A bolstering trance.* In a chapter retelling battles between two warlords (their names escaped her) it mentioned that followers of both camps lended their warlords power with a trance to connect their souls. The war on both sides focused on breaking the meditation as the path to victory and defeat.

Her master passed the story off as myth; the whole book was filled with balderdash, far as everyone believed. Stories for postulants and children. It was terrifying to believe half those stories held some truth if what once was could again be.

Her gaze passed back to the docks where the view remained clear. A blond man paced at the front, and if she hadn't seen Ivin Choerkin leaving on her ship, she might've sworn it was him. In his hand a sword like she'd never seen before, its length as tall as a man, but translucent as fine crystal. *Another myth from a dead age. Latchu.* In a matter of a couple weeks her entire perception of the world and its past had changed.

Sedut stood nearby, her hand aglow with the same power which had raised Ulrikt from the dead. That tidbit brought her tongue to her lip for a curious lick. *When and why the hells would Ulrikt have given that back to her?* The more she knew, the less she understood, or as her father once said: *You dig in the compost, you never know what kinda shit you'll find.*

She squinted at the scene, wishing her prayers for Life would let her see further with clarity; the waters of the bay looked turned to ice.

Ice. "Godsdamn."

Deelee tugged her dress. "What do you see? What?"

She squeezed the girl's hand and bolted for the eastern wharf with Deelee struggling to keep up. Shadows and Taken would die in water, but walk straight across ice; the boy's hiding place wasn't safe. Their path was clear until they reached the line of guards, and they slipped through without question.

They were halfway to the end of the wharf when a Shadow's shriek brought her to a sliding stop. Unless her ears failed her, the chilling cry came from in front of them, not behind. She glanced back at the hundred strides between her and safety, and a second shriek rose from the north. Another and another, piecing together in a song fit for the Slave Forges. The next scream brought her eyes to the gatehouse ahead, and atop the tower stood a Shadow.

"Run girl, back to the guards. Go!"

"No."

Figured that her new kin would be a brat, and there was no time to argue. She let go the girl's hand and ran, hoping she'd at least hang back, but footfalls drummed behind her; the Shadow leaped over the parapets, and instead of floating like a falling leaf as she expected, it fell with the weight of a man, but lit with the grace of a feline.

She spun around the end post of the wharf and gazed beneath into the rocks with her prayer-filled eyes. "Godsdamn!" A run for nothing; the boy was gone. She turned back to Deelee who'd fallen behind, waved. "Back! Run!" Damned if the girl didn't listen, or… she glanced over her shoulder and saw the Shadow gliding for her, and two more further behind. At least the girl wasn't so thick as to not run for her life.

Armed men and folks with buckets of water were only a couple hundred strides away, but those once beautiful lifesaving boots were weighting her feet down with drumming strides on the dock. She felt as though she were clogging along like a giant duck, and someone ahead must've decided she wasn't going to make it, as the wall of guards opened. A blond man and a priestess ran her way. Saved by a Choerkin and Sedut would embarrass her face to a beet red, but she didn't have the breath to cuss her shame.

The Choerkin chambered his sword over his shoulder for a strike that made her question if he came for her head. "Slide!"

Legs burning from calf to thigh and breath gone it took a flicker to register, and she dropped to her hip in a slide as the blade flicked past her head in a near invisible swipe. She rolled to her back, casting her eyes back in time to see the crystal sword cleave a perfect streak through the Shadow. The thing stopped as if it'd hit an invisible wall and shrieked, but its death was less a horrifying wail and more dying whisper. Then it disappeared as if never there.

A half dozen Shadows stood statue still as she lay panting on the dock's worn boards. The man stood guard over her as she came to a knee, and a glance to Sedut spoke to why they didn't attack: the woman stood in a swirl of frightening energy with dancing surges that mimicked rotating blades. No way in all the hells anything would meet her willingly.

The Choerkin gave Meliu his hand, lifting her to her feet. "You're well?" This Choerkin sure wasn't Ivin; he had a smile and way to tame a wild spirit. Or, her childish grin was because he'd just saved her life.

"I'm alive, thank you."

"Good."

And he shoved her toward the line. She stumbled and ducked her head as she passed Sedut, but it didn't appear the high priestess looked at her, let alone recognized her.

Deelee rushed in to clamp both her legs before Meliu could brace, and she damned near toppled. She clutched the girl's head in a hug to her hip. The girl cried and Meliu laughed.

"What the hells were you doing out there anyhow?"

The Choerkin bore a scolding gaze, and she couldn't help but giggle. But the giggle died, and so too her smile. "Looking for a boy under the dock, he was unconscious, I hid him there. He was gone."

"So many people missing others. My kin are smoke now, but at least I know where they are."

Meliu blanched and stared Deelee in the eye rather than catching his. "I heard. I'm so sorry."

"You know me? I doubt I'd miss such a pretty lass in town."

She dipped her head and blushed. "Not your name proper. But, you're a Choerkin, you remind me much of Ivin."

"You know my cousin. My name's Eredin."

"Well met, sir. I am Meliu. I met Ivin in Ervinhin not far back."

He nodded, face grave. "Ervinhin… I'd heard hope of most escaping from there." A dour frown sank the corners of his lips.

"We may look alike, but Ivin is the better man. If your life needs saved, trust him before me."

She smiled, but it didn't get the rise from the man she'd hoped. "It was you who saved me just now."

"You were the lucky one. I… must be going." His face grew darker, and the way he cast his eyes to the cracks in the dock suggested he recalled some blood-soaked memory. "Stay near the guards from now on." His smile was weak as he walked away, but at least it'd returned.

Deelee punched her in the hip as he disappeared in the crowd. "He's an alley cat, and every girl in the Fost knows it."

"I bet it doesn't stop 'em." The girl pursed her lips and planted a foot. "Don't worry, sis. We're getting the hells out of here on the first boat I find."

* * *

Raised near a spine of mountains in a mining camp didn't prepare Meliu for the creaking scramble of boards some fishermen called boats, nor what variety of filth captained them. Reputable vessels were full or suspicious of strangers, in truth most were gone already, and the tubs which remained wreaked of profiteering. Several larger ships, and a dozen square-sailed raiders, bobbed in the open waters of the bay, clear of the peninsula of ice, but they were Choerkin controlled. She considered tracking down Eredin and flirting their way aboard a skiff to one of these ships, but then if those same ships went into battle?

Better to die dry.

She plied her and Deelee's tale to sailor after sailor, with no small number of whimpers and tears from the girl, but unless her tears were gold Meliu figured not a one would pay their sorrow no mind. One woman spat in her face when she offered a hundred songs for passage, but most turned their backs with a snort and dismissive wave. If she threw on her priestess' robes might buy a favor, but just as likely they'd squeeze her for every song she had or thought she had. Prayers and wealth were what priests were known for here on the docks.

Meliu set eyes on a three-masted ship, also bristling with a bank of oars, mooring at the furthest western dock. It was a breath of hope until she noted the swarm of souls as desperate as they were waiting on the dock already. More would follow swift as swallows. "Hurry."

Deelee's feet carried her faster than her short legs would suggest, but everyone always underestimated Meliu too. A man's voice rang out as they approached: "We've space and supplies for a hundred, and that's piling the mule's back! A hundred, no more! A short trip to the Watch, and we'll be back to load as many as we're able." Sailors lined the rails of the ship, each armed with an axe, cutlass, or bow. "We keep it tidy, the cap'n points to you, you board. Any other catches an arrow!"

Pleading shouts and angry curses answered, but no bowstrings sang. People were filing aboard by the time they reached the line. Meliu's heart beat and it was hard as hell to keep her feet still. There were more than a hundred in front of them, but while the Captain fingered men, he weighted boarding toward women and children; if they'd arrived quicker, they'd be on deck. *Damn every moment I spent haggling. I'm two steps behind.*

They jostled and bounced as folks pressed in from the rear. Meliu lifted Deelee onto her shoulders. "Count." And she figured it didn't hurt to raise a youngster to the Captain's eyes.

"Ten already on deck… maybe? Close."

"Keep counting."

"Seventeen. Twenty-five."

Meliu's knees buckled when kneed from behind, and she stumbled, but kept the girl aloft.

"Thirty-seven, now forty?"

Meliu nudged a dozen steps closer, close enough she caught glances of the Captain through gaps in the crowd. Clean shaven, broad shouldered, and ordinary as any man except for his broad-brimmed hat and authoritative stare. She also caught the name of the ship, *Januel's Grace*, but a swath of fresh black paint streaked across the letters as if someone had grown unhappy with the name.

"Fifty-five, sixty."

So damned close. Her shoulders and spine ached, and she swore she might be a finger shorter by the time they made it to the Captain.

"Seventy. Eighty. We ain't gonna make it. Ninety, maybe more."

Meliu's thighs burned and her knees quivered.

The Captain's voice was higher than the sailors. "You there! The very tall lass. Forward."

A gap opened, and she stared straight at the captain and the gangplank.

Deelee's knuckle rapped Meliu in the forward. "He means us."

Meliu was too exhausted to blush at her foolishness. She took a single step and dropped to her knees, and Deelee bound toward the gangplank.

The sailor spoke. "They'd make a hundred and two, Cap'n."

The captain stepped to block the girl. "Sorry lasses, I said a hundred and meant it. If you're still here when we return, you'll be the first aboard."

"Please, sir. Our mother..." Meliu realized she was on her knees and it might appear she begged, so she stood. "We were separated from our mother." Meliu took Deelee's hand.

Deelee added, "She's on the blue-folks' ship, already set sail for the Watch." Tears streamed down her dirty face.

"With the Luxuns, you say?" The Captain's gaze softened, but after a glance back at a deck stuffed full as a can of snuff, he shook his head. "I am sorry." He stepped onto the gangplank and stopped to address the people aboard ship, "Before we depart, are there any holy onboard to save a soul?"

Meliu glanced about, there wasn't a habit in sight, though there were plenty who might use a healer. *Why now? Why at all?*

"A healer I say. Do me this favor and its double rations. Any holy at all?"

Deelee tensed in Meliu's grip, and she let go, backhanding the girl's shoulder. The child glared, but kept her mouth shut when Meliu shook her head. Something didn't feel right, even as the crowd grew restless behind them.

Things could get bloody quick, and she didn't understand how or why the tension grew palpable in the shiver across her shoulders.

A voice came from midship. "I can heal some."

No, don't, but she couldn't put word to why.

The Captain stood on his toes, nodded, pointed to a sailor. "Bring him here."

"Aye, sir."

The sailor lead a man to the Captain. He was maybe thirty and clad in simple trousers and long coat, and it took a good stare to put a name to him through the beard. *Simund.* He'd left Istinjoln several years past to serve at the Fost. *Please don't recognize me, don't give me away.*

Simund smiled at the Captain. "Who might I assist?"

The Captain turned to Meliu and Deelee. "These two young ladies. Way I figure, a godsdamned priest would eat and drink more than two girls."

A cutlass split the back of Sigmund's skull and a sailor shoved him into the bay in front of a silenced mob. The Captain stepped from the gangplank and gestured. "After you, ladies."

But Meliu's feet froze as Deelee stepped forward and tugged for her to follow. The Captain's eyes were emotionless, cold as a shark's.

"Mother will be at the Watch waiting. Come on!"

The desperate, pleading eyes of the girl's gaze edged Meliu's feet forward. If she boarded, if she refused, either way she could be the next chum in the water. "Mother's waiting," she mumbled. Her eyes fluttered as she struggled to smile at her new sister, but as she crossed the plank, she couldn't manage a smile for the Captain.

She tried to escape him once aboard, but the man followed her until she reached the main mast and turned to face him, sliding Deelee behind her.

"What?"

"I'm Captain Lodol." His bow was curt, and she didn't return the honor. "A religious girl are you?"

The conversation's direction poked her gut from the start. "I always figured I was no more religious than the next, but seems I was wrong."

"Istinjoln unleashed this horror—"

"I fled Ervinhin to find my mother and sister in the Fost, don't tell me about horrors."

The squint to his stare suggested she'd dented his confidence. "Ervinhin. Aye, I'm sorry for that." He shifted his feet. "Did you see the people behind you? Hear them? Feel them?"

"They were angry because you killed an innocent man. A holy man."

His words came fast and terse. "No! They were angry before I killed a holy man, and no godsdamned holy is innocent."

"You could've fit us both aboard."

"Yes."

Her fury built. "Yes?"

He took control of his tone and pace as if explaining to a child. "If I'd taken you aboard, I'd have broken my word of one hundred and the woulda rushed us. Hells, if I left you they mights done the same. I split one son of a bitch's head and saved a dozen more from arrows and drowning."

"It was wrong."

"We aren't arguing about right or wrong, girl, I'm just telling you what is. And I well might've saved your hide." He spun on a heel and bellowed: "Cast off! Man them oars and get us the hells out of here!"

It pained her to watch the stares from the docks; a flicker before, she was one of them. Oars splashed and the *Januel's Grace* put water between ship and tears, but not a soul made a move to jump.

Captain Lodol might've been right, or might've been wrong, but either way he was a mean bastard. With the caveat he'd gotten the two of them off Kaludor. Her mind struggled to reconcile her spite and gratitude, dropping roiling anger into the pit of her stomach.

Oars steered them to open water past the growing bridge of ice, and soon after sailors set to raising sails. Meliu stood with Deelee, staring back at the docks and the hulking Shadow posed as a looming statue.

Deelee said, "Thank you."

Wind struck the sails and they snapped, surging the ship into a rocking lean. It wasn't long before her anger emptied from her belly into the sea, and Deelee repaid her life saved by patting Meliu's back.

Waves surged and the boat rolled for what felt endless hours, and she'd never heard of a prayer to cure this seasick torture. Meliu also considered that a prayer might get her head split open, so she resisted the temptation with the promise from so many that her reeling gut would go away. It didn't. The roil subsided a touch, but the essential misery of it all stuck to her innards like a bad batch of her pa's cheese sauce. The one made from mare's milk.

The memory damned near drove her to leaning over the rail again, but she sat still with eyes clamped shut.

A throat cleared, and Deelee nudged her ribs. The Captain stood over her when she dared open her eyes. A steaming cup of something was in his hand.

"We call this Storm Tea, normally we reserve the drink for rough seas. But seeing as I just saved your life, I figured it rude to let you die on my deck."

Meliu took the cup with shaky hands, caring not a wit for the burn on her fingers. "Thank you."

The Captain nodded, handing her a ceramic jar. "Honey to help make it go down. Need more tea, just let me know." He strolled away as she brought the tin cup to her lips and blew steam.

Storm Tea tasted like mint crossed with chewing on a branch of cedar, but with honey enough to turn it into syrup she quaffed all but a few gooey drops to settle her stomach. The ride after was misery still, but she survived until her sea legs arrived on the second day afloat.

She avoided speaking to everyone but Deelee the best she could, but the girl had too much fun telling everyone about how her sister from Ervinhin found her after all these years. Trouble was, all Meliu knew of Ervinhin were from fevered days hugging the *Codex of Sol* while under the watchful gaze of the Wolverine. She set nary a foot outside the inn… except to visit bodies.

Her hatred of sailing came in handy when folks tried to talk to her. She claimed an unease in her belly, puffed her cheeks with a cough, and anyone nosey left her be without testing her knowledge of the village.

For two more days she drank thick tea, ate what little they offered, and slept beneath the stars on a rolling hardwood bed. She awoke to a joyous call from sailors: "Herald's Watch!"

Meliu's eyes were open, but still Deelee shook her, bursting with an annoying level of child's excitement. "We're here, we're here!"

"I hear, I hear." She uncurled from the deck to sit, but couldn't see a damned thing other than people's legs, so she stood. And couldn't see a damned thing other than people's shoulders. She grabbed her gear (including cup and honey) and squirmed between folks until finding a view. "Unholy hells."

Herald's Watch rose several hundred feet above the waves of Purdonis Bay, with a great tower at its pinnacle, but its majesty didn't keep her eye; hundreds of vessels, ranging from fishing boats to cogs, surrounded the island, masts swaying as they packed tight throughout and around the tiny harbor. People moved to and fro, tiny from this distance, bringing to mind maggots swarming a crumpled corpse, the tower a dagger in the dead's back.

Seven

Ugly Bird's Tears

What dance can't you learn given time?
Ritual or fun, humility, prophetic, joyous,
each culture to its every own,
foot stomp, hand clap, whoop yell and clasp!
The Dance universal, unlearnable, but which any may perform: Dangle Dead.
Which cracks first, branch or spine?

—*Tomes of the Touched*

It took a day and a half from dropping anchor for Meliu to reach dry land. She figured the dock was sturdy enough to weather the mightiest storm, but her smile waited until her feet settled on stone. Her body relaxed as if it were the first time she'd breathed in days.

Then she overheard a nearby sailor: "Aye, we'll be making sail for Skarmak soon as able, no way this 'ere tiny rock feeds all these folks long."

Meliu grimaced at the prospect of trudging back onto a boat, despite the extra tea and honey she'd stowed in her haver. She hugged Deelee and caught a whiff of the girl. Then she considered it might be her own reek, or maybe the collection of hundreds packed around them. "Now we're off the boat I can smell again… We need a bath, child."

Deelee cocked her head. "Days of whining about water and now you wanna climb into some?"

"Hot water, with soap. Scented if we can find it." The girl's nose and lips curled into a snarling grimace. "You've never had a proper bath have you?"

"Bath houses are for high folks."

Meliu leaned in and whispered, "And the holy." She stood and glanced down the wharf for an inn, but saw nothing. "Steaming water and perfumed oils can change lives, at least for a time. You're my sis now, time you learn of a few of the finer things." *But where? Skywatch, I'm bound to know someone there.*

Her first-hand knowledge of Herald's Watch rivaled her first-hand knowledge of most places: a rough a sketch formed from the pages of books, and most of them lacked detailed maps. She knew one useful thing: Skywatch was a domed building built from white marble, she'd didn't spot it from the boat, but it'd be damned near impossible to miss if she got close.

This meant marching her stiff, exhausted body uphill, into streets notorious for their climbing and winding nature. She took Deelee by the hand and lead her northwest toward where she thought she spied towers belonging to a gate.

They were buried in the crowd for a slow and brutal hundred strides before the masses thinned and she could see a gate clear as the sun above. Either something beyond the gate smelled worse than they did, or there was some other reason folks avoided its open portal. It might have something to do with a dozen armored guards with spears and shields.

She nudged Deelee to smile as they approached, and Meliu greeted the head guardsman, his helm with a horse's tail dangling down its back. "Good sir, I require passage to the towers."

Eyes surveyed her from dark shadows behind his nose-guard. "You've a writ?"

"No, sir. I met Ivin Choerkin in Ervinhin a couple weeks back. He was headed for Istinjoln. He'd be pleased to see me again, I'm sure of it." She flashed an innocent smile, but one which held a curl of mischief. She hoped maybe the guard would think the Choerkin smitten with her.

"Kotin Choerkin was murdered, poisoned, and the eldest son may yet die, I doubt he's much interested in you. Move along."

Her brow scrunched; talk about a plan backhanding you. "I've just now made dock from Kaludor, pray, what happened?"

"Ain't your godsdamned business, is it? Move along."

She straightened her spine, set her jaw, and lied through her teeth. "Ivin Choerkin and I are friends, what harm in telling me a truth?"

"The truth? The truth is a Forge-cursed monk poisoned Kotin Choerkin, Tokodin by name, and his head adorns a pike not far from here. And therefore, not a soul passes without a writ."

No. Her shoulders slumped as the air left her lungs. *Impossible. Tokodin was never a killer. Never.* Her mind raced. She could tell the truth and damned near guarantee passage straight to Ivin: In chains. No way to know from there if the Choerkin would free her hands from those chains, or her head from her body.

"In that case, you need let me pass. I didn't want to speak thus in front of so many but… I also met Eredin Choerkin at the Fost, and he gave me this." She produced Ulrikt's scroll, and motioned for him to lean in close. "He found this on a priest thought to have some hand in Lovar's murder."

She made sure the broken Church seal was visible, and the man's hand reached for it in a lurch. "I'll deliver it straightaway."

But her hand was quicker than his. "It is my charge, sir, and you'd do well not to mention this to no one."

"An escort then."

"Too much attention, we've already drawn too many eyes."

He stared at her, then the Lord Priest's seal. "Go then. But if I find you played me, it'll come down hard on you."

Meliu bowed, her face stern, then strode through the gate with Deelee in tow. They passed through the tunnel, and once on the other side the girl looked up at her with a smile. "Sure you weren't bred in the streets?"

"The tunnels of Istinjoln can be as conniving as any street."

Her moment of victory was short lived, her mood overtaken by word of Tokodin's end. She wouldn't have believed such nonsense if she hadn't seen Tokodin on the *Entiyu Emoño* with Ivin a few days past. Believed he'd been accused of murder and executed, that is; she would never believe his guilt.

The streets here were quieter than near the docks, and she snagged an elderly passerby with a pitiful glance. "Where's the head of the bastard who murdered our Lord Choerkin? I wish to curse his soul in person."

The grizzled man snarled, "The head," and pointed northwest. "Follow this road yonder to Longyard Street, due north, you'll find 'im."

Meliu walked with a snap to her step, half dragging the girl.

Deelee asked, "Why d'you wanna see a head"

Meliu snapped back, "Because I knew that head, now shush."

They found the decaying trophy of Tokodin's life impaled high on a wall overlooking a small square where several streets met. The wings of a crow framed the face from behind, the animal flapping to keep its perch in hair, and the head wiggled as the bird pecked at remnants of an ear.

"That's your friend?"

"Yes." Even staring at his dead face she wanted to believe it wasn't him, but the scars marking his cheeks made reality undeniable. His eyes were holes and dried blood mimicked tears from his sockets. *How could they believe you a murderer?*

"He makes for an ugly bird."

Meliu flinched, and she was half a breath from backhanding the urchin before she thought better. If she was more like her father, Deelee would be sprawled on the ground, weeping or unconscious. "What godsdamned right you have to say such a thing?"

Deelee glanced at her, shrugged. "It's true."

Meliu picked up a couple rocks from the street and was proud as the heavens when one struck the crow's head on only her second throw. The bird squawked and flailed its wings, but landed no more than five paces from the head to wait for them to leave.

So much death, so much pain. Tokodin's end struck her, but not so much as she'd expected. Anger. Confusion. Pain. No tears. A month ago she would've blubbered as a child. The Fires of Tezmonu had hardened her soul with the pains of living, before now she'd not known for sure what that'd meant. Survival trumped all other cards life could play.

"Let's go, sis."

They continued north until finding an open shop. They stepped inside and walked out with a new pack for Meliu, a pouch for Deelee, and directions to Skywatch.

* * *

Priests guarded the doors of Skywatch, and Choerkin warriors stood geared for a fight at every corner around the temple. Choerkin eyes made her nervous, but the priests at the door stood calm and cast polite smiles as she approached. She tilted her haver for a glimpse at her hidden robes and whispered, "Priestess Meliu of Veleen."

A priest knocked on the door and it opened on silent hinges.

Deelee gasped and yanked at Meliu's dress as they entered, staring at the perfect night sky above. Meliu'd read numerous tomes with descriptions of Skywatch over the years, so she figured herself prepared for what she'd see; she was wrong.

A million stars, more clear than a dark and cloudless night atop the Tower of Sol shined down upon her. Her mind reeled as it struggled to comprehend eternity. Until a voice broke her stare.

"By what right do you enter Bontore's temple?"

Meliu lowered her eyes to gaze on a priestess with a familiar voice. "Temeru of Himden?"

Silence, then a smile. "Meliu of Veleen?"

Meliu left Deelee staring at the stars as she trotted to embrace one of her oldest friends. Their birthdays were only days apart, so their bond as children never broke, despite Temeru's study in the Way of Bones. "I thought you served in Movan?"

"I did, but they moved me here not long after." Temeru eased from Meliu's hug, her face worried. "You shouldn't have come here."

"Where the hells else should I go? Shadows and Taken, Kaludor is lost."

"Not here. A monk murdered the Lord Choerkin, and High Augur Meris… They say she jumped from the Watch—"

"Meris!"

"Dead and burned to the sky, but I say someone threw her. But she wore a monk's habit as if to disguise who she was."

"She oversaw the Night of Bones in Istinjoln… Now she's dead—"

Temeru's quizzical stare stopped Meliu's words. "That's impossible, she never leaves these stars."

"No doubt, it was her." The priests here were woefully behind on the stories from Istinjoln.

"There were a few days I didn't see her, but… No matter." She laughed, the inflections making clear she was unconvinced. "There isn't an adherent safe on this island. A mob hanged three monks two days past."

"But you're safe here."

"Yes, the Choerkin promise our safety, within these walls. But, no. Those with the long vision say the ice is coming, and on it rides evil."

It was hard to believe the Shadow's power capable of freezing a bridge so far into the bay, but she'd seen so many things she'd never imagined, she'd feel foolish questioning her words. "We'll stop it, somehow we must." Everything she'd witnessed argued against her statement, but she needed to believe.

Temeru's eyed widened and she leaned in. "You were at the Crack of Burdenis? Is it true the Shadows struck the shrine first?"

Meliu sighed, she didn't want to answer. She didn't want to remember. "Yes. It's true, then Istinjoln, but Lord Priest Ulrikt sent me to the Fost hours before they attacked." Before the summoning? The hells if she wanted to discuss details and speculation.

"You've seen them, then. Wait, Ulrikt sent you?"

Meliu pulled the scroll from her haversack and handed it to her, pleased to be rid of the damned thing. "Sent me with this message, for High Priestess Adelin, he claimed."

Temeru unrolled the scroll, sucked her breath. "Priestess Meliu..."

The woman's formal tone caught her by surprise, as did the lavender hued glow of her face.

Temeru turned the scroll for her to see, and in place of "Flee Kaludor" were the words "Sail to Tomarok" in flowing script with a light purplish glow.

"My dear, you're in the wrong place."

The air fled Meliu's lungs, her muscles giving way to weakness, but in a flicker she replaced the air with anger. She snatched the scroll from her friend and stormed to the door, shoving it open to read the scroll beneath the light of day. "Flee Kaludor. That son of a..." Deelee and Temeru stared at her. Still best not to call the Lord Priest names around living ears. "Where the blessed heavens is Tomarok?"

EIGHT

Person, Place, or Thing?

Chew the sand, slap the hand,
Breathe the foam from the loam:
Deadly Frog.
Witness the brilliance in the Dark,
Fright at the shade in the Light.
Shade, shadow, dark, oblivion, the void.
the Great Separator.
Impossible? Impossible. Possible I'm, says I.

—*Tomes of the Touched*

The library beneath Skywatch was well-stocked with the wisdoms of the augurs, but she figured the odds of finding mention of Tomarok were slim. Still, a tickle in her nose didn't put it past Ulrikt to leave some clue on purpose, so she climbed the stairs every day. She scrounged through bound tomes, loose pages, and scrolls, but not a single reference to Tomarok. When not reading, she listened to word from the outside world: Eredin had arrived to the Watch, but there wasn't even rumor of High Priestess Sedut and her artifact. More ships were leaving for the continent, and all attempts to stop the bridge of ice had failed, including One Lash's Fire.

The only good coming from their trip to this island was they both bathed daily with a quick trek across the street. Once Deelee smelled better, half the folks in the temple adopted her. One fitted her with robes, and soon after, adherents began calling her "Urchin the Pious." Deelee frowned at first, just like she did at smelling nice, but the moniker grew on her.

Then, official word came from the Choerkin: Abandon the island. Several priests vowed to remain behind in Skywatch to fight to the death; Meliu wasn't one of them.

The Choerkin promised to get everyone off the island, but promises weren't something she attached faith to these days. "If Tomarok is a place, the docks… the Luxuns might be the folks to ask, plus, I need to secure berth on a ship."

Temeru stood stoic, fingers entwined in front of her nose.

Meliu sighed. "I spent days without a soul knowing I was a priestess, I think I can survive a trip to the wharf."

"Skywatch has hired a ship with a captain we trust."

"And that ship is tethered to this island and surrounded by a hundred smaller boats. No offense, old friend, but I've seen more Shadows than I care to. Deelee and I will leave soon as I can manage."

Temeru exhaled her further protests, pulled a pouch from her robes, and placed it in Meliu's palm. "If you insist… As you travel at the behest of Lord Priest Ulrikt himself, the Temple of Skywatch feels a duty to assist in your journey. This should see the both of you to wherever Bontore directs your winds."

Meliu didn't open the pouch, but gave it a small squeeze; flat round coins, in addition to what must be cut stones. She smiled and fought tears as she hugged her old friend. "Thank you." She stepped back, glanced to Deelee. "I'll be back soon as I've something arranged. And I've spoken to the Luxuns."

"I don't like it. What if you never come back?"

The child hadn't been away from her side, even learning to read a little as Meliu pored over texts, but sometimes a little sister could be a pain. "I'll be back. Besides, you've a hundred sisters and brothers now." She rubbed the girl's head, inhaled through her nose. "Ahh! You smell so pretty."

Deelee slapped at her hand. "Shut yer mouth."

And the three giggled.

Meliu stepped into a chill, cloudy day wearing a dress and cloak, and her hair hung loose about her shoulders as any ordinary girl, but the pain of the lie sat in her belly. She might return, she might not. Everything depended upon what answers she found.

The docks swarmed with people, but there was a different music to the milling. The sound on her arrival had been chaos and relief and desperation found in the stomping of feet and shouts and cries and curses, of crates slammed in a hurry, dropped or thrown to the side. There were no fewer people now, but the notes struck were filled with order despite a thousand musicians. They passed supplies hand to hand with muffled grunts of exertion. The calls were polite, whether questions, answers, or commands. This swarm of people arrived as a mob, but departed as gears in a greater machine. An army without arms or armor, and if somehow given weapons to defeat both Shadows and Taken, Meliu didn't doubt for a flicker they'd retake their homes. But instead, this militia performed another time honored tradition in battle: Retreat.

She moseyed along the docks seeking the attention of any captain or ranking sailor who'd meet her eye, and by the time she walked halfway to the *Entiyu Emoño*, she resorted to holding aloft a coin. "A fifty silver-song for anyone with passage to Tomarok!"

The coin caught several glances, but only a single stare; a skinny captain of a skinny boat, and she wondered if it was seaworthy. "Aye, I can take you there."

She smiled and palmed the coin as he reached. "First, you tell me where it is."

The man guffawed and she moved along. Another captain, of a small but sturdy ship waved her over.

She asked, "You know of Tomarok?"

He wore a black mustache dangling to his sternum, and his grin sported a missing lower front tooth. His words carried a whistle when he spoke. "Can't say as I do, and I know me a thousand places. But I've space aboard and'll get you to the continent, damned sure."

"How long until you depart?"

"Be an hour, maybe, when a channel clears to get our oars out of here. Won't be too many boats safe fer a pretty lady all alone, I'll guarantee that."

She nodded, certain he didn't lie on that account, but she wasn't so sure how safe his boat would be either. "I may be back, Captain."

She gave him a curt bow and continued her journey to the Luxuns. Not another soul bothered trying to lie the silver from her fingers, nor offer her passage elsewhere. Whatever, wherever, Tomarok was, either no one knew, or they weren't willing to take her there.

The *Entiyu Emoño* sat loaded with crates, but the stacks diminished as supplies disappeared below deck like bits of food down an ant's hole. Captain Intœño stood staring at his sailors with arms crossed as if in constant judgement of their efficiency.

"Nonfoñu!"

He turned, eyeballed her, and the feathers of his head flared before he strode her way. *"Nonfoñu. Erbit entoñeo."*

She crossed the plank, stomach churning just to set foot on a ship again.

"I am well pleased to see you alive. Are you ready to embrace the sanctity of the Wave Dancers and join our crew?"

She glanced to the deck, confused. The Wave Dancers were the gods of the Luxuns, deities who took the form of dragons and other beasts to dance in the ocean's waves, but the question felt out of place. Meliu smiled when she deciphered his meaning: She wore a dress rather than black robes. "Sometimes a woman's piety needs hidden."

"Indeed! Yet, if you've come to claim half a keg of ale for your lost passage, I fear it sits in the bellies of my crew."

"Or pissed over the rail."

He laughed, a vibrato sound with a hint of trilling chirp. "Still, the ale was passage for two, if you care to join us we'll call a debt squared. I may owe you for how you amuse me."

She bowed deep, but she wanted to give him a hug. A clear channel lead from the docks to open waters for this ship alone, a gift by Choerkin decree if they needed to sail fast. She might have to hide if the wrong faces came aboard, but it'd be worth the price. "It would be a privilege. But I also have a question: Have you heard of a place called Tomarok?"

Intœño's right eye squinted. "-arok, not Tomlok?"

"Tomarok. But they could be the same. Words change when they travel."

"They do, they do. Tomlok is a city on the west coast of Northern Vandunez, an independent city of the Ayumbar Peninsula."

"You've been there?"

"Once only, a fortress-city of tan stone… You would think its people more peculiar than you find me." He grinned. "Does it sound like your… Tomarok?"

"I believe not. It could be an old word, the name may have changed… I don't know. But I've been told to find it, by an elder I suspect is dead now."

"The dead should leave directions, yes?"

"For certain. Would anyone onboard know?"

"You may ask as we travel, a few might know of places I don't."

She was no closer to solving the mystery, but passage on the *Entiyu Emoño* meant more than a fast voyage: it meant Deelee could join her in safety. "Would a fifty silver-song earn berth for a young girl?" She held up the coin with a grin.

The Captain snatched the coin from her fingers with a wry smile. "That's more profit than I stand to make for the next month, the way the Dancers align of late."

"When do you shove off?"

His head bobbed. "There is no hurry."

"The lady?"

He smiled and tapped his nose with her coin before strolling back to the stairs leading to the stern castle.

She wasn't a dozen steps from the *Entiyu Emoño* before a handsome man in his thirties smiled at her with a greased mustache above teeth whiter than the stars. "You asked of Tomarok?"

Her heart jumped, but an ill twinge struck her spine. The man's gaze was as slick as his facial hair. "I fear I gave up the last of my songs for space on the Luxun vessel." She took three steps past him, but he trotted until turning in her path. "Knowledge for free, miss."

She planted her feet. "Quit milking and pour the cream then."

He cast an abashed smile. "No, heavens take me, I know not a lick. The master of the *Fair Wind* sent me."

Not the captain, the master, the owner of the ship if she knew her dock talk. It did little to settle her unease. "Forgive me for not recognizing the name, I know more mountain trails than boats. And I won't meet no one who don't give their name."

"The mistress may slap me for saying… but, Shae Turvil. She owns three merchantmans, a finer lady of trade you won't find."

She walked around him, smiling, and engaging. "I've no longer a cause to find Tomarok, but thank you." Too damned convenient the master was a woman. She glanced into the crowds for any familiar face, in case the man persisted. Even a Choerkin would suffice, though she'd prefer Eredin to Ivin.

The man jogged to circle her again, his smile too broad, his bow too deep. "The master takes her invitations right serious, I beseech you to follow."

Her heart raced. A hundred people around them, what would he dare do by light of day? "And I beseech you to let me pass before I call the guard."

His voice lowered, but he stayed in a bow with a pleasant smile. "I could gut you and flee to one of a hundred boats to disappear." His hand snaked to her, and a prayer for Light to blind this bastard was on her lips, but his palm was open and empty except for a wheel of wax the size of a coin, its face stamped with a lion's head. It was the Seal of Istinjoln. The Seal of Lord Priest Ulrikt.

He'd struck curiosity to her gut, and didn't need to run. "Who is your master?"

"The lady, Shae Turvin. She wishes to speak, don't make me bleed such a pretty lass as you."

Meliu took the wax from his hand, peered close at its indentations. There was no mistaking the mark after carrying Ulrikt's scroll for so long. "If I scream, you believe you'll live?"

"Maybe, or not, but you won't."

Meliu clamped the seal in her hand. "Take me to this Shae, then."

He straightened with a jovial smile that lacked all hints of sinister from a flicker before. "The master was correct as always… mentioned you were a smart lass. Shall we? Name me Fedal, if it pleases you."

"Your blood would please me."

His smile grew happier still. "Exceptionally right about you."

"I've never heard the name, Shae. She knows me less than she thinks."

He rolled his eyes. "Oh! The master has many names." He offered his arm, but in jest, before strolling thirty paces and turning down a dock, but he made certain not to lose her no matter how slow she walked. But the seal assured she didn't want lost, she wanted time to think. Istinjoln lore spoke of one ring passed from lord priest to lord priest, meaning there was little way Meliu could conceive that this Shae wasn't linked to Istinjoln. Perhaps Ulrikt himself. Curiosity would drive her feet beyond the fear which raised bile in her gut.

Fedal's cocksure strides lead them to a cog with a massive, single mast. The *Fair Wind* bustled with sailors and passengers; it was clear the ship approached casting off, as smaller boats cleared a channel from the docks. The man stepped aside and gestured to the gangplank. When she hesitated: "Lass, you done came this far, and I'm just being a gentleman."

He followed her onboard, too close for her taste, but she gave him credit for one thing: The nerves he set on edge made her stomach forget it was on a boat. She squeezed the seal in her hand, surprised it didn't melt in her sweating palm. "Take me to this Shae."

Fedal scooted around her with a hop and a skip between crew. "This way."

Double doors with huge, but plain, brass handles barred entry to the captain's cabin beneath the stern castle, but they weren't locked, and Fedal cracked them enough for a slender girl to enter.

Her eyes struggled to adjust to the dim light of twin lanterns hanging from support beams, but when they did, she forgot to breathe. A figure draped in holy black robes stood with their back to her, and as the hooded cowl turned she half expected Lord Priest Ulrikt. But Fedal hadn't lied; the master was a woman with long black hair and a porcelain smile.

High Priestess Sedut.

"Meliu of Veleen. Welcome to the *Fair Wind.*"

The doors clacked shut behind her, and Meliu remembered to take a breath. And bow. "High priestess."

"My apologies for the awkward invitation. Wine?" It was less question than statement; she poured and handed Meliu a goblet as she gestured to a seat. She neither drank, nor sat.

"Your bastard threatened to gut me."

Sedut's right cheek wrinkled with a smirk. "He knows better. But I wanted you with me, and he got you here."

"High Priestess Adelin? Is she here as well?"

"With sadness, no. She died, but without being Taken, gods be praised for a single mercy."

Sedut pulled a chair from a table and sat in its plush velvet.

"Lord Priest Ulrikt's fate?"

"Who's to say? Like you, I was sent from Istinjoln candles before… whatever happened."

Meliu didn't trust a word the woman's tongue stroked so smooth from her lips, but a face so steady and relaxed was impossible to read for a lie. "Tomarok?"

"You tell me."

Meliu took a drink on that note, letting her fury settle. "You shittin' me?"

"There's the mining camp girl Ulrikt loved." The woman sipped from her goblet, and Meliu resisted the urge to slap it into her face. "Did you know Ulrikt, too, was born in the mountains?"

Meliu rolled her eyes. "Your man told me you know of Tomarok."

"He did. Please, sit and talk."

"Pound your words in the Forges, I don't have to be here."

"You should rest, clear your head before we speak further."

Meliu strode for the door but her knees buckled.

Sedut moved swift as a viper, but instead of a bite she nabbed the goblet from Meliu's hand as her knees struck the floor. Her thoughts clouded over, her eyelids were anchors, and instead of cursing her mouth surrendered to a yawn. There were dim flutters of light as a dull pain spread from the side of her head; a hollow thud and distant words fading into nothing were the last things she heard: "Slumber would've hurt less if you'd sat."

NINE

The Helping Hand

Sihodo reigned for a hundred years and fought half as many wars without losing one. There was a monumental secret to his victories which his enemies could never learn: He fought wars he had already won. Learn the truth of this wisdom and you too will stand resolute in the Conqueror Heaven.

—Codex of Sol

"You're awake, good. I'd begun to worry for you."

Meliu groaned, her body swaying but her stomach calm. Wrapped in blankets and hanging in a hammock, the image of being a spider's kill came to mind.

Sitting relaxed in a high-backed chair, with legs crossed, was the spider.

Meliu said, "What the hells, how long?"

"A day and a half, or thereabouts." Sedut held out a steaming tin cup. "Nothing nefarious, brewed from the tea in your bag. Ample honey."

Memories returned, foggy and vague, but she could swear Sedut never prayed to put her to sleep. "I didn't drink the wine… how?"

"The scent of wine covered Terem fumes, useful to remember in the future. I *do* apologize, but it simplified things."

Meliu struggled to rise in the hammock, got her bearings, and took the cup. She sniffed, eyeballed the high priestess, then drank. The thick concoction served to ease her hunger pangs as well as rising nausea. "This is the second time I've missed a Luxun boat. Where the hells are you taking me? Tomarok?"

"Where did you come by that name?"

"Lord Priest Ulrikt's scroll."

"It says 'flee Kaludor'. Oh, don't worry, all your possessions are intact, just not your secrets. Oh! And for your peace of mind, that child you drug with you from Kaludor sails with Temeru, though for a different destination."

She blushed, embarrassed that she'd forgotten Deelee, but pleased to hear of her fortune. But anger bubbled back to the top. Meliu grunted. "Secrets." She didn't have secrets worth keeping no how. Except the bag of coins, maybe. "If read beneath the stars of Skywatch, then the scroll says to sail to Tomarok."

The woman's brow furrowed. She was a plain lady, despite perfect raven hair and ivory teeth, and the look didn't suit her. "What ink does such a thing?"

It was a question which had vexed her scholar's mind, but she'd stumbled on the answer in the library beneath the stars. *A variant of Moon's Glow, fashioned from enchanted, and powdered, amethyst.* But she didn't share her wisdom. "Such lore is rare, but Ulrikt had access to histories I would never see."

Sedut waggled a finger at her. "You would've. He liked you, by the time High Priestess Demoy would've passed on to the stars, you would've been her replacement."

Those words rattled her brain. Demoy was the Lord Priest's Keeper of Lore, likely one of a handful of living souls to help translate the Codex of Sol and other forbidden texts. She'd never considered herself achieving such an honor. "You flatter me. If Demoy were here, she might've known what he meant."

"She doesn't." Sedut leaned, a hard stare straight into Meliu's eyes. "No lies. You've never heard the word before?"

"Never."

"I have."

The ship creaked and groaned to break the ensuing silence; if not for the fact Sedut could kill her with a word, she might've leapt from the hammock to give the woman a good shake. "Where is it then?"

"I don't know."

Meliu stared at the ceiling, rubbed her forehead, then took a drink of Storm Tea. "You are a useful one, ain't you?"

"Ulrikt tolerated your tongue better than I will."

"Save me from your threats… When, where did you hear the word?"

"From Ulrikt. Those privy to the words of prophecy mused on him becoming King Priest. He laughed and proclaimed king priests could only be crowned atop Tomarok."

Meliu's head spun, but she wasn't sure if from waves or these words. *A tome detailing the crowning rituals of king priests? What other secrets might such texts hold?* "Ulrikt knew things I don't."

Sedut clucked and rolled her eyes. "He knew more things than all of us. Many more."

"Atop Tomarok, a mountain? A hill?"

"Another time he questioned if it still existed. If maybe, like the gods, it'd been banished from the world."

Can a mountain be banished? Destroyed for certain. "Volcano?" A half dozen volcanoes lay scattered along the Estertok Range.

"I believe he meant more literal."

"You mean the Great Forgetting?" She'd seen charts kept by ancient mariners, they held little relation to recent maps. The oldest map she'd seen depicted the world with a single continent stretching around the world. Many claimed it a fantasy.

"I mean the First Forgetting."

Meliu sat up in the hammock, damned near spilling to the floor as it swung. "What the hells do you mean, first?"

"The histories teach us of the Age of God Wars, the Banishment, the Age of Warlords, and the Great Forgetting. Ulrikt believed the Banishment resulted in a Forgetting. You've heard of the *Fifth Treatise*?"

"Yes." A book of some sort, but nobody bothered to explain what it might be. "It mentions a First Forgetting?"

"Lord Priest Ulrikt often spoke of the maps in the Fifth Treatise when his mind wandered to history. The finest maps he'd ever seen."

"You're saying the treatise may hold Tomarok's location?"

"He couldn't send you to a place banished from the world."

Meliu drained the last drops of tea and eased her feet to the floor, her legs wobbly and weak. She plopped into a chair across from Sedut. "A problem for the Forges: Those maps are in the Library of Istinjoln, in a room hidden."

"No."

"No? You have it?"

"I spoke with Lore Keeper Demoy at the Fost. She secured the tomes of the hidden chamber before escaping."

"I need to find High Priestess Demoy."

"No."

"No?" *This woman's an itch between my shoulder blades.*

"There were two tomes missing from the library, the *Fifth Treatise* and the *Codex of Sol.*"

"So who do I need to find?"

"A dozen priests knew the location of the tomes, I will give you a list."

Meliu stood, swaying with the roll of the boat, and her Storm Tea stayed down. "That's a meaty stew you served." Then she spoke words she never imagined herself saying while on a ship. "I need to take a walk to digest it."

Sedut grinned. "You always did pace."

Meliu skulked to the door and gave it a shove, then turned to spew some nastiness, but nothing good came to her. "Shit." She had to be satisfied with storming out the door.

***

Three days sailing the Parapet Straits, and her lack of retort still burned her thoughts now and again. Worse, nothing she'd come up with since satisfied her neither. So she paced. A lot. But, it was Ulrikt who brought the fire from her coal with the mystery of Tomarok; Sedut acting like she knew her so well was just an excuse to be angry at someone close. However, knowing this didn't put out the fire, it pumped the bellow.

She leaned against the starboard rail gazing at another cog trailing them. The *Blue Dolphin* was similar in size and design to the *Fair Wind.* Four smaller ships sailed with them; Sedut owned the entire fleet under the alias Shae Turvin, a proxy for Istinjoln. The Church owning trading ships was another surprise in a world which had been turned upside down and twisted sideways, recognizable but different. She was out of her depth in all these goings on. Everything was simpler with her nose stuck in a book, reading of people long dead.

Scuttlebutt among sailors suggested they weren't far from land, so their eyes cast south often, but as the day wore on, storm clouds to the west drew more attention. They were dark and ominous, but seamen assured her they'd reach land before winds howled. She doubted their certainty, figuring they'd feed her these kind words to ease her fears even if about to be sucked into the depths by a whirlpool or eaten by some sea beast. Flickers of lightning in the distance caught her eye, but the next words she heard were more frightful.

"Sails to the prow!"

The cry from the crow's nest swept her eyes south, but the horizon was clear. She climbed the steps of the forecastle, and in moments Sedut joined her.

Meliu's fingers drummed a rail post that some bored sailor once carved into the head of a horse. "Trouble?"

"We'll know soon enough."

Flares passed, and the captain strode close, stretched a spyglass and stared. "There they are. Just come over the horizon. Tek for certain."

Sedut asked, "Heading?"

"Straight up our noses."

Sedut prayed. "I don't see a flag nor markers, to which of the hundred nations do these belong? Captain's an ugly, bearded bastard."

Meliu prayed, but as expected, her vision didn't stretch so far. "You're serious? You can see his beard? Can you hear them?"

Sedut prayed again. "I can hear when they shout. Tekite, but I can't understand them."

"I might, what the hells are they saying?"

"*Daet. Kouki. Soandol?*"

Meliu knew Hidreng best of the Tekite dialects. "Shittin' hells, they ain't Hidreng. Who else would be in these waters?"

The captain said, "Tek Brotna most like, but too many damned nations to list."

Meliu locked eyes on the deck, straining her memory. "Sounds likely, but several nations use the dialect."

"*Oxindo hetame*. A different voice this time."

Meliu's fingers tightened on the carved head. "What? You're sure? Turn sail now! Get us the hells out of here."

The captain turned to her. "Why?"

"Arrows and axes! I don't know much of the Tek Thon dialect, but—"

"A half dozen more sails!" The cry from the crow's nest set the hairs on her neck straight. "Platformed for war!"

The captain's eyes bore a fierce stare. "Thonians? You're certain."

"Those words, damned sure. Thon bears influence over several nations."

The captain turned to holler commands, but Sedut grabbed his shoulder. "Not yet."

Tek Thon was one of the most powerful of the Hundred Nations, and one of the most brutal. There'd be no mercy from them bastards. Escaping Shadows to run straight into Thonian arms tested her Storm Tea's efficacy. "What the hells are you doing? Warships! We need to run."

"No, you need to run. Captain, I want you to signal the *Black Owl*, they've a passenger coming."

Meliu met Sedut's gaze; the mirthful sparkle in the woman's eye made her queazy. "Oh, forges be damned, no."

* * *

It took two sailors to drag her into the rowboat, three to haul her there the second time, but the boat dropped too fast to escape for a third try. Once the hull plummeted and hit water all she could do was float and pray the effects of the Storm Tea didn't wear off. The bastards didn't even give her oars.

Within several flares the *Black Owl* arrived, a smaller, swifter, and more maneuverable vessel and they lifted her onboard with a hooked pole. They struck hard starboard the moment Meliu sat secure on the deck, sailing east.

The captain of the *Black Owl* was a man called Oash. He was young, brash, and full of vigor until he spotted Tek sails swerve to follow them. His vigor turned to vinegar and venom. "Whoresons! You better be important, priestess."

Me? For the first time in her life, Meliu figured she must be important, but gods be damned if she knew why. Either way, time to act like it. She straightened and glared. "Aye, I am at that, so you'd best captain this ship instead of flapping that tongue at your betters."

She strode straight past him to the aft rail without looking back, and there she stood for candles. Sails grew closer in a world turning premature dark, as the sun dropped behind black clouds flickering with lightning. To the port side she could see the coast of Northern Vandunez for the first time. All her life she'd stared at maps and wondered what the world was like off the frozen rock of Kaludor; she never dreamed of seeing it while fleeing for her life.

Night fell, and not a lantern nor torch was lit. Not even a pipe was smoked. Captain Oash was sailing blind, trusting the eyes of a priest to avoid land, reef, or another ship.

"Our enemies know these waters." He paced, repeating these words as if every hand needed reminded. "Damn, I'd like to be bare poles when that storm hits."

Meliu shook her head and walked away, praying for Light to settle her nerves. She sat with her back to a pile of rope and pulled her knees to her chest, convinced she might as well nap. She closed her eyes, and a massive roll of thunder didn't convince her to open them again. A flash of lightning lit her eyelids and its crack was so immediate she feared the mast struck. She looked up, pleased to see the mast and sail intact.

The starboard sky lit in a series of flashes, and she caught sight of a ship at full sail. She screamed, "Tek! North! Starboard!"

"Full sail!"

Streaks of light lit the sky and it took a flicker to register: flaming arrows. Several struck the deck, but she glanced to the sail, figuring it was the real target; it was whole, thank the gods.

The Captain belted out, "Hard Port!"

The man had lost his senses, port would lead them to land. She ran to tell him so. "What the hells are you doing?"

"Their depth of keel will keep them from the coast."

"They know these waters, what if it's what they want us to do?"

His glare was hard. "Your prayers will serve us better grounded than boarded, but pray for neither."

Flaming arrows streaked a lightning lit sky, but none hit deck this time. Maybe the captain was right.

"Rocks!" The priest at the fore ran toward them. "Dead ahead!"

Lightning ignited the sky and Meliu didn't need a prayer to see what lay ahead. Waves crashed white on jagged stone thrust from the surf, and the ship shook and leaned for a flicker as it clipped a hidden reef.

Storm winds surged, driving the sails hard.

The *Black Owl* shuddered a second time, and Meliu stumbled to keep her feet. She dove for the main mast, eyes wide, staring at an oncoming finger of stone. The boat's hull ground hard, and she felt the cracking of the planks as the ship lurched to an awkward halt, its mast damned near horizontal; screams came from all around and sailors and commoners alike careened into the surging waves of the surf, disappearing into the black waters like so many bugs tossed into a well of ink.

The boat leaned hard as winds and waves drove its boards crunching further onto the reef.

Meliu locked fingers around the mast and hugged with her legs to keep from tumbling toward the edge. A wave broke and washed over her, soaking her cloak into added weight. The night sky was lit by a score of shooting stars; flaming arrows hissed into the waters and thunked the deck, one passed through the remnants of the sail dangling below her.

She scrambled atop the mast and strained to reach the rail of the listing boat. Her fingers caught the edge and she pulled herself to its crown with a defiant scream. Glancing out to sea showed the faint silhouette of the Tek vessel lit by archers dipping arrows into torches. She leaped for the finger of stone and caught its side, scraping hands, elbows, and knees, but she managed to climb through the pain with clenched teeth.

She kneeled atop the stone as a second rain of arrows streaked through the sky, striking the *Black Owl*. They did little but add a glow to the night until one struck and flared into blinding white light. Meliu blinked and covered her face in the crook of her elbow. Heat swelled to warm her face and she lowered her arm to reveal a world of blinking blurs as her eyes adjusted.

An area the size of a shield blazed with crisp white flames; whatever the arrow carried, she'd never seen its like.

Shadowy archers in the distance ignited arrows, a couple of their faces already aglow from nocked flames; arrows soared in weighted arcs, and in a flicker she realized the burning boat lit her position on the rock.

She turned to a field of black, with no way to tell stone from water, and no time for prayer to light her way. She put a hand to her perch to find purchase for a climb, her feet skidding on the edge. *Jump*, but her body didn't listen. An arrow sailed over her head and sizzled into water, its blaze before death doing little to reassure she'd survive a leap. It wasn't with faith in the gods she jumped, it was a faith in odds, splash or crash versus burning arrows.

She sprung as far as wearied legs could launch her, aiming for the arrow's splash. She clenched her eyes tight, remembered to take a deep breath, and fell. Anticipated when she might hit. Flexed her knees.

Waters splashed.

Stone jarred every joint in her body and she lost her feet in the waves as she crumpled like a nail misstruck by a hammer, folding shoulder first into the surf. Salty water drowned her screams; she choked and gagged as she rose to her right elbow, her left folded against her chest. She tried to stand, but a wave swept her forward, so she crawled.

Something struck her in the sternum, and she flailed, imagining a poisonous sea snake as she'd seen depicted in old books, but instead she found an arrow with its tip wrapped in rag. She clutched its shaft and dared stand as the force of the waves lightened. She stuffed the arrow beneath the crook of her arm and hobbled forward, hoping she never need use such a desperate weapon.

She squinted as lightning lit the clouds: thirty paces to shore. The world disappeared from beneath her step and she plunged into deeper water. Her feet found bottom and she shoved off, resurfaced with a sputter and gasp, and paddled toward shore with one good arm. Words of prayer passed through her head, but opening her mouth brought water, and body and soul were so exhausted there was no way to know if the gods could answer.

Her feet kicked sand and she struggled forward quicker. She fought to stand when the water was waist high and two desperate steps later she collapsed, rolling to her back to keep from drowning. She lacked the will for prayer, hells, she lacked the will to drag herself from chill waters. The only will left to her was to lay there and die. Or live. Whatever fate long ago decided. She closed her eyes and just breathed.

Finger's clutched her right wrist, lifting her arm, dragging her from the surf and onto a pebbled beach.

She kept to her plan to die, breathing easy, her eyes closed, but she vowed her last action would be to plunge the Tek arrow into the eye of whatever fate this was.

The grip loosened and her arm dropped, and she snatched the arrow's haft, her eyes opening, expecting to find a dark eyed Tek looming. There was no one.

"A favor fair, is a favor repaid in kind." The voice was of a young boy, but the quote was from the *Book of Emhon*, a tome studied by venerated priests, not children. And sure as the hells, not by a Tek of any nation.

She rolled to her good elbow, pain surging in her other shoulder as she raised her head. A boy stood beside a small fire, poking it with a stick. She panicked, but her body couldn't respond in kind as she flopped to her chest. "Put that fire out! They'll see."

The child turned to her with a face familiar; days before, she'd carried him to shore. "Do not worry. They will not see a fire."

Meliu rose again, this time to her knees to crawl beside the blaze before collapsing. "How the hells are you here? I left you beneath the docks." Her face slumped into the crook of her elbow and she relaxed, relishing the heat of the fire. "This's impossible. There's no way you could be here."

The voice came deep and soulful, no longer a child's. "You were a hard lady to find." She raised her gaze to the child's same blue eyes, set atop the same child's body, but they rested in Lord Priest Ulrikt's face. "Sleep now."

Shriek beak,
glower in the green eye imprisoned black,
Eagle, Owl, Falcon, or Crow…
the Raven, don't you know?
Of course, of course, sentimental me.
Supplemental deterioration of detrimental interrogation,
secondary, tertiary, quaternary.
Nary a thought to be had to matter to the most,
to the host, to the living and breathing Ghost.
What say you to the vivid Dreamer,
the chaotic Weaver,
the false Believer,
the true Deceiver,
the Ghosts who see you as the dead and decayed.
What word have you, to deny reality's greatest lie?

—*Tomes of the Touched*

Foreword to Hiding Fire

Hiding Fire was written well after the first draft of Eve of Snows was complete. I wrote it for several reasons, but the key driver was to get the story out of my brain.

In early drafts of Eve of Snows there was a prologue that took us back to the time Eliles met Ilpen, and of course, Ears and Ears. As the story blossomed, it became apparent that the prologue was unnecessary, so it got the axe.

But, after Eve of Snows was complete, I had a reimagining of the story based on the opening line. About that same time, I felt the urge to write a short story (which is something I am not a fan of, to be blunt) and this fit the bill. I had also been discussing various point of view strategies for the writer on a fantasy forum, and it occurred to me that I had never written anything in first person.

Hiding Fire, then, is the result of Eliles' backstory kicking around in my head, merging it with the twisted urge to write a short story despite not liking short stories, and to do so in First Person when I don't much like reading first person.

In the end, Hiding Fire was something of a challenge set for myself… aka, short story torture.

I hope you enjoy.

Hiding Fire

"Little girls don't survive in the woods."

Those were words my mama hammered into my head from the time I first toddled, and tempered with tales to keep my feet from the underbrush.

I never saw no wolf, though I heard them singing some nights, and the witches were rarer still. But I believed. The woods terrified me, and I clung to mama's hem every time we drew close.

I was five years old when she took me to them same woods in the dead of night. She kneeled, grabbed my shoulders, and looked me straight in the eye. "Run, Eliles. Don't let your father and them priests catch you. Run! And never come back."

I cried, argued, stomped, then I ran. My feet wanted to make a big loop, take me home to the only place I ever knew. My child's mind tried to convince me I could hide under the floorboards, find comfort in the sound of their voices even if I could never let them see me again. The animal inside me knew I needed distance and shelter to survive.

I ran until my lungs gasped and my legs dropped from beneath me. I crawled under the prickling branches of an evergreen, a cedar by the scent, and pulled my blanket tight around my shoulders, the only feel of home remaining. I rocked and sobbed and muttered: "Not my fault, the fires ain't my fault."

It was a lie, but truth gave me no peace.

By the time my tears dried a pack of wolves yapped a frantic song to the west; papa once told me the unnerving yips and barks marked excitement after a kill. I didn't know whether to find comfort in their bellies being full, or fear they were so close. I drug myself to my feet and walked opposite the terrible sounds until my legs would carry me no more. I squirmed through the branches of another cedar and climbed to find my bed for the night.

Winter was fading into spring, but I could see my breath cut by the needles of the tree. My fingers grew cold clutching branches, with only thin wool gloves covering my hands. My little friend arrived without my invitation; warmth seeped through my blanket and clothes between my shoulder blades.

"Go away. I don't need you." I spoke to them often, but never knew if they listened, or if they were alive in a way I understood. Sometimes they obeyed, sometimes they didn't, just like the head strong cur who wandered the streets of the village sniffing for handouts.

The warmth disappeared, but it didn't leave. My friend hovered before my eyes, invisible except for a ball of wavering mirage about the size of my fist. It was warmth within reach, comfort, but it was also the reason I dangled freezing in a tree to start with. The night grew colder, my lids heavier, and my fingers weaker. Clouds crossed the stars and promised rain. My anger at my friend faded with practical considerations.

It wasn't the flame's fault that Bunter and his horse-faced mother saw me with fire sitting on my finger like a baby chick.

Burning their barn down was another matter, but didn't something in the back of my angry head ask for that too? I'll admit, years later now, to such a notion.

I whispered, "All right, just a little fire."

The wavering mirage turned into a wick's flame hovering in the night and I grasped it, the glow turning my hand red and showing off the bones inside. It didn't burn, it was a fluttering heat that eased the ache in my joints and spread through my body. I closed my eyes, savoring the moment, forgetting the glow spreading from the cracks between my red fingers.

"I've spotted her!" A lantern in the distance cast shadows of a hooded man in dark robes. Hounds bayed further away.

My heart stuttered into a race, and I descended quicker than intended, crashing through branches the last several feet. I landed hard on my rump, jarring my spine to my skull. My friend went dark, but I could sense it by my ear as I rolled from beneath scratching branches and ran. I took the advantage of my short legs in the underbrush, ducking and weaving through gaps a big man couldn't fit.

I cursed myself for a fool as I ran, recalling a tale papa told often about a brush with bandits and its obvious lesson: You can't hide fire in the dark. My mind raced, searching papa's hunting tales for lessons recalling wily critters that escaped him.

The big man ripped through bushes and vines, lumbering my way, crashing and cursing in the names of all the Twelve Hells. Slipping through the brush I was quiet and quick, but he was powerful and determined. I glanced back, the light of his lantern growing closer, and the world dropped from beneath me. I fell, tumbling with snags of roots and broken branches. I sprawled face first beside a stream, and hope flashed, but I wasn't some fox able to survive a swim in icy waters. The banks were too wide for me to jump, my lungs burned, and my body ached. If the hounds caught me, I might be torn to shreds before an inquisitor had the chance to cleanse my soul for the Seven Heavens.

I rolled to my back, lantern light casting shadows over the ravine's bank as the holy approached. Priest or monk, it didn't matter. He was the inquisitor's man. I'd run further, but I'd never escape their long legs. I imagined picking up a stick and fighting back, or my friend burning this man to cinder. It was a flicker of a thought.

Fire lit my face and streaked through the night quicker than a diving hawk and struck the holy as he reached the bluff of the ravine.

I jumped to my feet.

His robes caught fire.

Flames and shadows and shrieks.

"No! Don't kill him!" I sprinted into the dark and in a flicker my friend was again by my ear.

Shouts gave us chase. "I'll kill you, witch! Kill you myself!"

I can't say if insight struck then as I ran, or later as I wandered: Mama sent me into the woods because it's where she thought I belonged, where the wolves and witches live. If given a chance, I might've thanked her later, but I'd never have forgiven her.

The rains came after, washing away tears and pursuit. The trees thinned and as the sun struggled to light the world behind heavy clouds, I stumbled into open ground gone soggy from the downpour. The heat of my friend gave me warmth against soaking cold as it snuggled under my coat where I could stick my hands. I swiped streams of water draining over my brow in rivulets and wrung my hair.

The great forest I'd always imagined had come to an end, and as I looked back at the woods, a little of its mystique died. But it still held death, and it hunted me.

I slogged forward, the ground sucking at my boots 'til I came across a wagon rutted road that was little more than two streams of mud with a grassy island running its middle. Roads lead to people, safety or doom, but my stomach growled. I followed right, taking me further from the wood.

I saw the donkey's ears first, then heard the cussing. A big man stomped around a wagon, its wheels stuck in the muck. What he lacked in furor he made up for in creativity. "Son of a turd sucking toad poker!" He stopped to stare at me when he realized he and his two-donkey team weren't alone. His hands went to two knives at his belt. "Where the Twelve Hells did you come from?"

I stared, a drenched kitten uncertain whether to purr or dash. Instead, I sobbed, shaking, on the verge of dropping to my knees. He raised his hands from his blades.

"I'm sorry, girl. Weren't meanin' to scare you." He walked slow, kneeled, and hugged me. It was a soft man's move, if I had a dagger even a child could find his kidney, but his gentle nature broke my fear and I leaned into him. "It's all right, child. Ain't gonna hurt you. Nobody will, not now."

I sniffled. "Eliles. I'm called, Eliles."

He looked into my eyes and his nose crinkled, a corner of his lip lifting into a grin. "Your eyes are so brown, like my youngest, Zezze." It was peculiar, my eyes are blue, but it made no sense to argue, and the man faded into his thoughts. "Consumption took her and her brother some time ago… But that ain't no conversation for a rainy morn, eh?"

I shook my head and he lead me to the wagon. Biscuits with honey butter was a feast finer than I'd ever tasted. Ilpen was a tinker, his wagon full of copper ware and tools of his trade, and his tongue was full of glib words for a little girl lost.

With me at the reins encouraging Ears the Elder and Ears the Younger, we got loose the mud as the rains passed, but as the wheels rolled, I couldn't escape the question.

"What's a wee girl doing out here alone?"

I sat as still as the buckboard allowed, wheel mill turning in my head. "I'm an orphan."

He kept his tone tame as if speaking of a joke rather than serious matters. "If you were an orphan, you'd know that ain't story enough."

"I just was." Ilpen might've taken my lack of answer with a dollop of patience, but on the horizon men milled on horseback. I squinted but couldn't tell who they were. "I need to run."

Ilpen slowed the wagon. "You run and they'll see."

His arm swung over my back, he fiddled with a latch and lifted a door covering the wagon's cargo. I slipped inside, elbows and knees rattling cups, plates, and other goods.

Running, hiding, climbing, falling in the woods terrified me, listening to the gentle clack of a latch locking me into a box sent spasms through my spine. My bladder swelled, more full of a sudden than when my cousin Tinle and I wagered the last hard-honey on who'd sit the longest. A silly memory, and maybe that was its point.

I breathed deep and clinched my knees, praying to Januel, goddess of love and war to save me, even if it were the servants of the gods hunting me. The wagon wobbled and banged on rocks in the road, and I held tight as we climbed the hill. I squirmed to a beam of light, peeping through a crack beneath Ilpen's creaking weight.

But the splatter of hooves on wet turf came from behind. "Ho, merchant!"

I daren't move, but oh how I wanted to find another hole to look through. There were three horses, maybe four.

Ilpen said, "I ain't got time, no offense mind. I'm on road to Coerkin Fost, and then to Istinjoln, and I lost a week with a broken axle not far back."

"We seek a girl, a youth."

Ilpen chuckled. "You've found the wrong sort of wagon for those tastes, your holiness."

A horse stepped in front of the wagon to force Ilpen to pull his reins. All I could see was a leg in black trousers,

"I trust you aren't a man to hide a child wanted by the Church."

"That's excellent, you'll be out of my way then, before more rains come."

"You'll be opening that wagon." I no longer feared for only myself, my fire would get this kind man killed.

"Right you are! In the Fost and Istinjoln, feel free to follow me there, until then…" Ilpen snapped his reins and the donkeys fidgeted, but the horse didn't budge. "Now gentlemen, I've entertained your little stop, but the Church has no authority on these roads, as it were."

"An inquisition carries the authority of Sol, king of gods." I knew little of Sol or the gods, my family had never been pious folks, but I did know the power of prayer. I'd seen wounds knit before my eyes and a man turned into a blithering dalcop because he dared insult a priest. Some holies even commanded fire through the power of prayer. If these holies turned the power of the gods on this man, his two knives might never leave their sheaths before he fell.

Ilpen's voice raised, I figured in desperation or fear. "Were we in Istinjoln I'd succumb, but this road is kept by Clan Choerkin." I thought to call out, admit to my fires and pray with the inquisitor for a safe trip over the Road of Living Stars before my execution. And I would plead for this man's life. But the words choked in my fear dried throat.

Not for an instant did I think the tinker knew what he was doing until I heard hooves coming down the hill, spreading to surround the wagon.

The horse blocking the road pranced, perhaps as nervous as me.

"Ilpen of Esteden, is that you?"

"Aye, I were in a hurry 'til interrupted, too. How's your bride?"

The holy in front snarled. "This is business of the Church and Istinjoln."

But the new arrival ignored the man in black. "Dead. For three years."

Ilpen answered, "Sad news. No new mistress?"

I couldn't tell how many new riders had arrived, I was guessing six, but I had no way to know. Papa always said a holy was worth two swords, maybe more, with their prayers. Voices were tight as bowstrings but the words remained pillows. I wondered how many men would die today because of me.

Saddle leather creaked, but I didn't see a thing. "Little Sister here is the closest to my heart, but despite her name, she's more a daughter to me. Only sixteen and she can put an arrow through a wolf's snarl."

A woman chimed in. "You've caught the Wolverine in a good mood after a rain, normally I'm the brat lass."

My heart thudded and my eyes flicked back and forth nervous with hope. Everyone knew of the Wolverine, head of the Wardens, whose word carried the law of the Choerkin themselves.

The man in black spoke, "Inquisition's been chasing a defiled girl since last night."

"Hear that, Little Sister? These two-faced boys huntin' a girl for using magic just like them." There were chuckles all around, saddles groaned and horses stomped. It was an unbearable insult, comparing feral magic to prayer. I couldn't see the rage, but I knew the tension pushed toward blood. There was nothing for it now, not from me, that would stop it. It was a strange relief.

The man in black's voice was stern. "We saw a passenger—"

The Wolverine said, "My friend Ilpen says he ain't seen no girl, he ain't seen none."

Ilpen spit, the buckboard rocking as his weight shifted. "Nothin'."

The inquisitor's horse turned to face the wagon straight on. "That a fact."

The Wolverine said, "It is now he done said it."

Little Sister whistled and giggled. "See there how easy that was? All settled."

A queer silence fell: nothing creaked or groaned, and not even the animals twitched. I didn't know what came next, a storm or warm breeze.

The inquisitor's legs squeezed his horse and moved him from the road. "I look forward to shopping your wares in Istinjoln."

Several horses departed, and as men chuckled to celebrate the passing tension, the Wolverine said, "You're a helluva tinker but a damned poor liar."

"What, you got an interest in some poor girl too?"

The Wolverine guffawed. "You think I give two pisses about some defiled lass?"

The latch rattled and the lid lifted to reveal Ilpen's grin. "Come on out, girl."

I crawled from the dark surrounded by a dozen Wardens bearing expressions ranging from disinterest to nervous. The Wolverine grinned through a thick black beard, a barrel-chested man in his forties covered in mail and a bear-skin cloak. "What're ya girl, four, five? Pretty li'l thing. So what'd ya do, heal your ma's cyst or some such?"

I shrugged, wishing for something so kind. "Uh-huh," I said, but my eyes burrowed holes in the ground. I was a worse liar than the tinker.

"Be honest, girl. I ain't killed no priest 'cause they can pray, I ain't gonna hurt a child for nothin'."

"Fire," I blurted, and hid my face in Ilpen's side, peeping at his reaction.

The Wolverine straightened his back and his brow arched. "When you're sixteen look me up, child, we could use you in the mountains come the winters."

Men laughed, but I looked to Little Sister. She was a slender gal with a round face and crooked nose, but pretty in her way. She smiled and winked at me before addressing the Wolverine. "We'd best ride with 'em back to the Fost."

The Wolverine nodded. "Hear that boys? Little Sister already runs this outfit."

After the humor passed the Wardens spread out, six to the fore and six behind. I glanced to Ilpen, he hadn't a word for me yet, and I had no idea what the man thought of me now. "Thank you."

He grunted. "You shoulda told me."

I didn't doubt he was right. "I'm sorry. There wasn't time."

"There were time, don't be tryin' to hornswoggle me again, you hear?" Silence stretched for what felt an hour, more, before he spoke again. "Ain't no way I can take you on as my own, you know. Inquisitors don't give up so easy. Fire, you say." All I could do was nod or shrug as he talked. "They'll hunt you down and kill you, they claim to find all them defiled by the vanquished gods. Hard to hide, I'm supposin'."

"Papa always said you can't hide fire in the dark." Defiled? I didn't believe it when the inquisitor spoke them words, I didn't believe it now. I'd heard the phrase in stories told by my folks. The vanquished gods, defeated in the God Wars, cursing mortals with unholy feral magic. "I ain't defiled, the fire's my friend, that's all."

He snorted and we rode without words, the song of hooves and wheels, creaking boards and saddles, our accompaniment. Until Ilpen hollered to the Wolverine. "We need to cut straight away to Istinjoln."

The broad-shouldered man turned in the saddle. "The monastery? You looking for a reward or somethin'?"

"Whoa, hells no." Ilpen turned to me with a smile. "The best place to hide fire is in fire."

I didn't like the notion of riding to Istinjoln Monastery any more than being outcast from my home in the first place. Less in fact, but Ilpen was dead convinced it'd keep me safe.

Six Wardens, including Little Sister, her real name was Puxele, rode escort north to Ervinhin, a village nestled in the foothills of ice-covered mountains. Here I hugged Ilpen and his donkeys goodbye as they continued on to Istinjoln. I wouldn't see him again for a year and a half, and every year after during the festival of the Eve of Snows.

After a month in Ervinhin, where everybody came to know me as an orphan, a local man called Serik escorted me to Istinjoln. The monastery was an ancient fortress, with towers higher than I'd dreamt, and a great portcullis to keep invaders and riffraff such as me out. My guide introduced me as his orphaned cousin, the gates opened, and minutes later a priest in black robes greeted me, his hood lined in red silk. He was a man in his fifties with a gentle smile filled with yellowed teeth.

"You're from the tinker's village?"

I knew then I'd met the man intended. "Yes."

"Good! Follow me, dear."

His hands slipped into the bells of his robes and he took me to a small building. A woman in a monk's brown robes opened the door as we approached. The room was bare, lit by a single lantern. He turned to me, his face grave. "My name is Dareun." He looked me over, and I quivered, ashamed. "Are you certain you seek the priesthood?"

I shrugged. I didn't, truth be told. "I could try to be a holy."

Bushy brows over gray eyes showed his mirth. "Your first lesson is that the followers of the Pantheon of Sol are called adherents, not holies."

I nodded with an embarrassed grimace. It was a silly word, I'd much rather have been called a holy.

He bowed his head, his lips moving in prayer with a mutter I didn't understand. He reached out and a ball of fire appeared in his palm. I felt its warmth in my spirit, not just on my skin, and smiled at him for the first time.

"Go ahead, Eliles. You're safe."

My little friend brushed my hand before igniting, circled the priest's fire before dancing in and out of its flickers.

"Fascinating." Not a hint of fear wrinkled his cheeks. My flame went dark and disappeared, and his prayer followed suit. "Before I decide, I must hear your story."

I looked into Dareun's solemn eyes through my tears and recounted my tale as I have for you, but in the words of a child. Instead of cursing me to one hell or another, he smiled. "You've the green eyes of my sister"—peculiar, seeing as my eyes are blue, but I didn't think to argue—"which softens a man's heart. I've watched a hundred children or more marched through these gates by inquisitors to be cleansed of their sins with not a one ever leaving, and each left a pain in my heart. Your father was correct, it's impossible to hide fire in the dark, and Ilpen too showed simple wisdom, fire may be hidden in fire."

He stood and clutched his hands behind his back, gazing on me from high. "But fire in fire may burn doubly hot, killing us both. Are you prepared to bear the heat?"

My first memory was of fire and heat, the tickle of its playful licks on the back of my hand. And what choice did a little girl have? "Yes. Are you?"

He chortled and mussed my hair, and I loved him from that moment. Neither of us could've imagined the prophetic in his words, but I suspect neither of us would've chosen a different path.

THE SUNDERING THE GODS SAGA

EVE OF SNOWS
MELIU
TRAIL OF PYRES
SOLINEUS
CITY OF WHISPERS

Join the Sundering the Gods Newsletter At:

www.LJamesrice.com

Signed Editions Available at L. James Rice's Facebook page, or email: LJRice@SunderingTheGods.com

If you enjoyed Meliu, please consider leaving a review at your favorite online retailer.

www.ingramcontent.com/pod-product-compliance
Lightning Source LLC
Chambersburg PA
CBHW030427310726
48979CB00009B/1654/J

* 9 7 8 1 7 3 2 4 0 8 3 4 0 *